Melodee began to laugh, but then stopped. She stared Fabi in the eyes, as if trying to drill a hole to the truth. "All right," she said with a nod. "You think your quince will be better than mine? It's on. You and me." She pointed to Fabi. "We'll have a quinceañera competition. And everyone here will vote."

Fabi felt the blood drain from her face. She never wanted a quinceañera in the first place. Now she had to have one — and not just any quinceañera. Fabi had to have the biggest, best quince the Valley had ever seen.

border town

Crossing the Line

Quince Clash

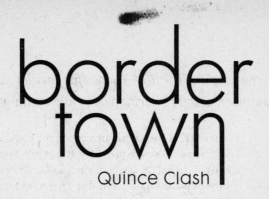

border town

Quince Clash

MALÍN ALEGRÍA

Point

To the people of the RGV. Thanks for your love and support, and for sharing your valle conmigo.

No part of this publication may be reproduced, stored in a retrieval system, or transmitted in any form or by any means, electronic, mechanical, photocopying, recording, or otherwise, without written permission of the publisher. For information regarding permission, write to Scholastic Inc., Attention: Permissions Department, 557 Broadway, New York, NY 10012.

ISBN 978-0-545-40241-5

12 11 10 9 8 7 6 5 4 3 2 1   12 13 14 15 16 17/0

Printed in the U.S.A.   23
First printing, July 2012

No todo lo que brilla es oro.

All that glitters is not gold.

chapter 1

Santiago Reyes knew he was pushing his luck. But whenever he drank, he had to pee a lot. Maria Elena begged him not to go, but Santiago couldn't hold it any longer. Finding a restroom wasn't too difficult. The tricky part was getting back to her room unnoticed.

He leaned out of the bathroom, straining to listen for any sounds. The restroom, like the rest of the extravagant mansion, was furnished in Louis XIV–narco chic decor. There were Roman-style pillars chiseled with Aztec snakes, a marble-top sink, and a heart-shaped bath-tub. Santiago listened to the pitter-patter of water from the interior waterfall and to the soft snoring sounds from the many bedrooms. Finally, Santiago emerged from the restroom, wearing nothing but his boxer shorts. He flicked off the lights and waited a moment for his eyes to adjust to the darkness. Santiago used his hands to help guide himself to the end of the hall and turned left. *It was left, right?* he wondered as he retraced his steps back to Maria Elena's room.

Maria Elena Diamante was a cute thing, with her soft wavy brown hair, dancing eyes, and sassy hips. Santiago had a weakness for women in tight jeans and high heels — the higher the better. But those girls were usually trouble, and Maria Elena was as dangerous as they get — in more ways than one. Her father, Juan "El Payaso" Diamante, was a known smuggler.

There were crazy tales that tied El Payaso to incidents of beheadings and torture south of the border, but Santiago had met the man on a couple of occasions and he seemed like such a friendly teddy bear with his family.

Santiago tried the first door and it opened easily. Soft snoring came from the mound on the bed. Maria Elena must have fallen asleep, he thought, carefully making his way toward her. She'd snuck Santiago into the house while her parents were getting ready for bed and he had promised to be quiet. But the excitement of messing around with her while her parents slept a few feet away — mixed with beer — gave him a sense of boldness that bordered on recklessness.

He jumped on top of the mound, straddling her body between his thighs, and bent to kiss Maria Elena on the mouth. But when his lips felt coarse hairs from a thick bushy mustache, he realized his big mistake. Or maybe it was the deep male voice screaming loudly that tipped him off? A figure beside Santiago rose up and shrieked. But the woman next to him wasn't Maria Elena. It was her mother!

El Payaso's shock gave Santiago a few crucial seconds to jump off Maria Elena's dad and run into the hallway. Santiago spun around, heart thumping wildly, hands clamming up as he hurried down the corridor, trying to backtrack. But he must have taken a wrong turn — *another* wrong turn — because he had no idea where he was. Luckily, Maria Elena swung open her bedroom door, eyes wide with surprise.

"What took you so long?" she whispered, pulling him into the room quickly.

Before Santiago could explain, there was pounding on the door.

"Maria Elena!" her father called out in a loud authoritative voice. *"¿Qué demonios está pasando aquí?"*

Maria Elena shoved Santiago into her closet. She hastily grabbed his clothes off the floor and flung them at him.

"If you value your life," she whispered in a dead-serious tone, "you won't make a sound." Maria Elena shut the closet door in Santiago's face. He fell back, banging his head against a dozen coat hangers with flashy dresses. His big clumsy feet trampled over pointy heels, bunched-up panties, and tossed clothes. He reached for his cell and texted his cousin, praying that she was awake.

Through the door, Santiago listened to Maria Elena talking to her dad. Sweat dripped down his forehead, stinging one eye. He strained to hear their conversation over the thumping of his heart.

"Did you bring a boy into our house?" her father growled in Spanish.

"Daddy," Maria Elena said, acting shocked. "What are you talking about? I didn't bring no boy here. I wouldn't do that after the last time. I was just studying."

"You take me for an *idiota*!" her father said, coming into the room. "Some punk jumped on me and tried to kiss me!"

"Are you sure it wasn't a dream?"

"A dream? *¿Estás loca?* I know what I saw. There was a boy and he was on top of me!" Santiago could hear everything clearly now — Maria Elena's dad was just outside the closet door.

"Okay, Daddy, calm down," Maria Elena said. "I'll tell you what really happened. But you have to promise you won't get mad."

Santiago's heart sank.

That's when Santiago realized that his luck had finally run out. *Can't trust no woman*, he thought. *Maria Elena set me up. She must still be sore about me taking her cousin to the dance last week.* His whole life passed before his eyes, even though he hadn't lived very long yet. He thought about his funeral. His mom, *tías*, uncles, and cousins would be so pissed at him for getting involved with a *narcotraficante*'s daughter. He should've known better. Grandma Trini would probably strangle his corpse to make sure he was really dead. And his mom would have to marry that loser vice principal just to move out of town.

Santiago heard the moving of furniture. Was Maria Elena's dad looking for him? He swallowed, knowing that he was going to be caught and that would be the end. In a last fit of desperation, Santiago grabbed his Virgen de Guadalupe medallion and prayed harder than he'd ever prayed before in his life. He swore to give up women and alcohol and go to school and even to class. He'd even go help his *tía* and *tío* at their restaurant, if only La Virgen would save him from ending up with two shots to the back of his head in some dirty ditch.

The doorknob started to turn.

"Dad." Maria Elena's voice grew loud and desperate. "It was Gordo."

The room became very quiet. Santiago leaned into the door to hear better. He heard her father say in a surprised voice, "Your brother?"

Santiago held his breath.

"Yes, he's back. And he was drunk. I threw him out. He was making such a ruckus. I can't believe you slept through that. You know how he gets when he drinks — all kissy and lovey-dovey."

Just when he thought he might be saved after all, Santiago's phone started to ring. It was so loud he swore the whole neighborhood could hear the bumping reggaeton ring tone. The closet door swung open. El Payaso Diamante stood in front of him, wearing nothing but a white T-shirt and zebra-print briefs. The look in the drug dealer's dark eyes was pure rage. Maria Elena's father was incredibly muscular, like a wrestler, from the waist up. Waist down, he had short skinny chicken legs. But Santiago only had eyes for the baseball bat in El Payaso's hands.

Maria Elena screamed and jumped on her father, who seemed to lose his balance. They both fell to the floor. It gave Santiago a second to leap from the closet and out the door.

"Run! Run!" Maria Elena cried.

In the hallway, he bumped into her mother, who was wearing a sexy nightgown. She screamed, horrified, and her glasses fell off her face. Santiago realized that he was half-naked, but there was nothing he could do about it, so he continued down the stairs and toward the entrance door. El Payaso released a string of curses behind him. Santiago didn't look back. He heard the family's dogs bark as he slammed the door. He wasn't sure if they were tied up or coming to maul him into a pulp. Santiago swore at himself for getting into this mess as he ran across the lawn, barefoot and wearing only his boxers. He knew he couldn't outrun the dogs. Suddenly, the sound of gun-shots burst into the night. His heart jumped. Santiago glanced over his shoulder to see three figures standing by the lit-up entrance of Maria Elena's house. Her place was way out in the boonies. No one would find his body unless they knew where to look, and that would only be after all the coyotes and birds had their way with his corpse.

Suddenly, Santiago saw the headlights of a truck coming toward him. He hesitated a sec-ond. Maybe Maria Elena's father had called for reinforcements? Would he be gunned down out in the open? But then he saw the worried expression of his cousin Fabiola Garza staring back at him from behind the wheel. He wanted to laugh out loud, but then he heard the hair-raising growling and snapping of the dogs.

Santiago put his hands on the fence gate and pulled himself up.

Before he could jump over, Santiago felt a sharp, searing pain on his left buttock cheek and cried out into the night. It felt like a knife had carved right into his butt. With all his strength, he pulled himself over the fence, landing hard on his right foot. Santiago's legs gave out. He couldn't get up. Fabi was at his side, along with her little sister, Alexis. Santiago looked up, gasping for air, into Fabi's big brown eyes, sunbaked brown skin, and dark hair that she always wore tied back in a messy bun. He winked. The two girls rolled their eyes and half dragged Santiago back to the truck.

"We have to take him to the hospital!" Alexis cried in near hysteria as Fabi started the truck. "I think he's going to pass out. Oh, my God! Do you think the dogs bit him? He could have rabies."

They were barely onto the road when the truck stalled. Fabi swore under her breath. She turned the ignition key again, but the truck only jerked and bounced abruptly. Fabi thought about where they were. They were ten miles northeast of the town of Dos Rios, out in the middle of South Texas open country. There was nothing but thirsty dry land, thorny brush, and mesquite trees. Another gunshot rang out in the night. No one would hear them scream, she thought.

"Try it again, Fabi — that guy has a gun!" Santiago shouted, as if she didn't know all this. "We gotta go!"

Fabi hit the steering wheel with the palm of her hand. "*Okay*. I heard the shot, too. Don't make me nervous. I'm still learning how to drive stick shift, okay?" Fabi tried again. Suddenly, the truck sprang to life, and she shifted the clutch into first gear. They drove away from the lit-up house, gunslinging father, and bloodthirsty dogs as quickly as possible.

Santiago awoke lying on his stomach at the Starr County Medical Center. A heavy book smacked him on the head.

"Hey! What was that for?" Santiago cried, stretching his neck to see who had hit him.

Abuelita Alpha, his cousins' grandmother, stepped into view. She was a petite woman who carried the fury of God and the devil in her eyes. Her soft white hair contrasted with the pale wrinkled hand waving a thick leather Bible wildly in the air. "*Niño malcriado*. That's for scaring the hell out of us."

"*Ya déjalo*," his grandmother Trini interrupted. "The boy is fine. That's all that matters now." Grandma Trini leaned over to play with Santiago's curls. Her face was made up as if she'd spent the night at a dance club — a look completed by her animal-print sequined halter top, ruffled miniskirt, and heels. "Here, *mijo*," Trini continued, "I heard you lost your clothes someplace, you naughty boy." She pulled out a bedazzled checkered shirt and glittery jeans. "They used to belong to your grandfather, but you know how everything old comes back *de moda*. I did the sparkles myself. Nice, huh?"

Fabiola couldn't help but laugh from the opposite side of the room. Her cousin Santiago was always getting into some sort of mischief. It had only been a couple of months since his court hearing, where Fabi had to prove his innocence so he wouldn't be charged for the muggings he didn't commit, and go to jail. Santiago swore that he had learned from his mistakes and promised not to get in any more trouble. Obviously, Santiago had a short-term memory. Lucky for him, she was around to rescue him — again.

Santiago looked at the shirt and turned to Fabi for help. When he realized that Fabi wasn't going to say anything, he smiled at his grandmother. "Oh, thanks, I love it . . . but I don't feel so well. I think I may need to stay in the hospital. I just went through a vicious attack."

Fabi walked over to his bed and raised two fingers. "Two stitches. All you got were two stitches from the dog bite. You were crying like a baby and telling us your last wishes."

"No, I wasn't." Santiago pushed himself up to his elbows. The bandage on his butt was showing through the opening of the hospital gown.

Fabi turned to her sister, who was smirking at them both from a chair next to the bed. "Alexis, tell him."

Alexis sipped on a cup of weak hot chocolate. She was still wearing her favorite pink heart-print pajamas. Everything about Alexis was petite and cute. "Yeah, you made us promise to donate all your clothes to the church. You told us about the five hundred dollars stashed away in your closet that you wanted us to give to your mom."

Santiago's eyes widened.

Grandma Trini smacked him. "I thought you said you had no money. *¡Mentiroso!*"

Alexis laughed and went on. "You wanted us to give locks of your hair to every girl in your phone book. And you promised me and Fabi your Pokémon card collection."

Santiago shot out of the bed. "Now I *know* you're lying. I would never give you two my collection! That stuff will be valuable one day on eBay."

Alexis smiled guiltily. "I just thought I'd add that little part."

"Ha!" Fabi pointed at him. "You're obviously well enough to get up. So get dressed. We can't afford this emergency visit. I told the nurse that we found you on the street and that you were homeless. Hopefully they won't charge us." She looked at the door as if she expected the cops to walk in at any moment to make them pay the bill.

Santiago buttoned up the flashy shirt and tight jeans. He posed playfully like he was a model. As the oldest boy cousin, he got all the attention growing up. It didn't help matters that girls went gaga for his dark curly locks and mischievous smile. It just encouraged his crazy behavior, Fabi thought.

Grandma Trini clapped cheerfully as Santiago dressed, then tossed him a pair of snakeskin boots to complete the vaquero look.

"Ay, mira," she purred, elbowing Abuelita Alpha. "So handsome, no? He looks just like Alejandro Fernandez."

"But shorter and dumber," Abuelita Alpha added, frowning with her arms crossed in front of her chest. "We better go before the nurse comes back and wants us to pay for the plastic water pitcher and cups you have in your purse," she added to Grandma Trini.

"I didn't . . ." Trini blushed. *"Ayyy,* well, they don't need it anyway. They have so many. They won't even miss it," she dismissed, holding tightly to her big, sparkly bag.

Fabi stood at the entrance, looking down the hallway. Was everyone's family this crazy? "Okay, guys, the coast is clear. Let's go before anyone notices."

The five of them walked out of the clinic. At four in the morning, even that large a group didn't stir up much notice, especially when Santiago's glittery cowboy attire was all the rage in South Texas.

But they didn't quite reach the door.

"Excuse me!" a nurse called out, catching up to them outside the lobby. She was a young Filipina woman with an accent. Fabi and the grandmas smiled and acted surprised. The nurse handed Santiago a clipboard with the release forms that he had to sign.

Alexis pinched Fabi softly on her side. "You always assume the worst," she whispered.

Fabi hated to admit that her little sister was right. She did always assume the worst. But she had good reason. Every time life seemed to go her way, like her quinceañera trip to New York City, someone or something would happen to ruin her plans. Although Fabi had forgiven her little sister for getting her in trouble, their father still held Fabi responsible for her sister's actions. Her dad was big on building character and believed that sacrifice and hard work were the keys to success. That's why he kept Fabi close to his apron strings — as an example. Now there was definitely no chance that she would go anywhere for the remainder of her teen years. Fabi was counting the days until she graduated high school and went away to college.

But for now she'd settle for getting out of this hospital and back to bed.

chapter 2

Something was up. Fabi felt the hairs rise on the back of her neck and shivered, even though the school marquee told her it was 90 degrees. That couldn't be a good thing, she thought. She watched in shock as Santiago grabbed his backpack from behind the car seat and followed Alexis and her into Dos Rios High School. The parking lot was crowded with trucks and SUVs parking or dropping off students. Usually, Santiago had some excuse as to why he couldn't go to school. But this time, he climbed the steps with them. He smoothed his curly locks out of his face as if he were nervous about something. Was he called in and going to be suspended? she wondered.

"Where do you think you're going?" Fabi teased.

"Where does it look like I'm going?" He blushed. "To school. I'm still a student, you know. At least, I think I still am."

Alexis saw a bunch of her friends gathered by the big fountain (which never worked) and ran over to them excitedly. Fabi couldn't help but be happy for her sister's renewed popularity. For a while, Alexis had been taunted and bullied by a couple of football players. They called her a slut and bragged that she did all kinds of freaky things to them. Alexis's ex, Dex Andrews, had not only tried to ruin her reputation but had also tried to frame Santiago for a crime he didn't commit. But when Alexis helped Fabi prove Santiago's innocence, everyone at school realized that Dex was a lying bully. His family quietly transferred him to a military school near San Antonio. Alexis was remarkably thick-skinned, and in no time at all, things had gone back to normal.

Fabi and Santiago continued their walk into the school together. Just inside the doors, Fabi turned to her cousin, who had stopped abruptly. He looked a bit overwhelmed by the crowd of loud, unruly students in the hall. She was not used to seeing him like this. Santiago was normally a smooth, borderline cocky, charismatic trendsetter.

"You okay?"

Santiago gave her one of his disarming smiles. "'Course I am. It's just been a while, you know, since I've been here so early. I think I forgot where my first period is." He laughed at himself.

"Santi!" a chorus of girls called out at once. The cousins turned to see three girls rush up toward them. It was Violet, Mona, and Noelia. The petite trio was dressed in matching preppy outfits and flower barrettes like some girl band. In a flash, their hands were all over Santiago, playing with his curly locks and touching his arms, back, and chest. The three girls had been friends since elementary school. Even then, the three were boy crazy.

"Did I hear you say you're lost?" Violet said, touching his arm.

"Don't you remember that we have home-room together?" Mona cut in, elbowing her friend.

"I'll take you," Noelia piped up as she slipped her arm into the crook of Santiago's arm.

"I'll take you, too," added Violet, taking his other arm. Noelia and Violet led him down the busy corridor as the bell rang.

"Hey," Mona called after them. She turned to Fabi and inquired softly, "I heard that Maria Elena was sent to a convent in Monterrey. Is it true?"

Fabi shrugged, smiling to herself. Everything was definitely back to normal.

At lunch, Fabi caught up to her friend Milo in the lunch line. Students were skipping ahead of him, but he didn't seem to mind or notice. Milo was not from South Texas, and it was obvious by the way he dressed in his oversize coat, Adidas sneakers, and retro red glasses. He was nodding to himself, lost in his own world, totally absorbed in some new song he'd found, and bouncing softly to the beat. Fabi grabbed him by the shoulders and shook him.

Milo smiled, pulling out his earphones. "Hey, you have to listen to this song I just discovered by this French DJ. Check it out."

Fabi held the headphones to her ear. The music was fast and good for dancing, with electronic beats. But it also sounded like every other song Milo raved about. Her stomach started to growl. "Hey, let's get lunch before they run out of the fruit plate."

They grabbed their trays and headed to the food counter. Fabi turned away from most of the cuisine: chili cheese nachos, chocolate chip cookies, mac and cheese — Milo's favorites. But Milo was a short skinny kid who never gained a pound. Fabi was into eating healthy. She wished they had a salad bar like at her best friend's high school. But Georgia Rae was in McAllen, a real city. Dos Rios was a decade behind the rest of the country. They were surrounded by farms and had a large population of migrant workers who worked the fields up and down the country, but there was no place to buy organic produce in the neighborhood. Being a vegetarian was a constant struggle at school and at home — especially since her family ran Garza's, a traditional Mexican restaurant.

"Daddy said I can have a quinceañera if I really want to," an annoying voice said behind her. "We already booked the McAllen Convention Center. And my dress is *so* cute. You're so going to love it. I designed it myself. It's a black-and-white strapless dress. My mom got the best fashion designer in Austin to make it. He was real expensive. But my mom says you only turn fifteen once."

Fabi didn't have to turn around to know who was behind her. Melodee Stanton, head of the Dos Rios dance squad, was the most annoying girl at school. Her horde of worshipers swore her tweets were gospel. Fabi had hoped that their relationship would improve after Melodee (secretly) helped her prove Santiago's innocence earlier that fall. But Melodee was on no one's side. She only cared about herself. The best thing for Fabi was just to stay away from her. Besides, Melodee *enjoyed* making other girls' lives miserable.

Fabi leaned over the counter. "Excuse me," she said to the lunch server. "Is there any more of the cottage cheese and fresh fruit platter?"

"Fresh fruit?" Melodee echoed mockingly behind her. "Some people just don't know when to give up."

Fabi jerked back. "What's that supposed to mean?"

Melodee continued talking loudly to her friends, ignoring Fabi's comment. "If I looked like that, I'd just stop eating, period."

Fabi could feel tears welling, but she held them back. That's exactly what Melodee wanted. She enjoyed pushing people's buttons. It gave her power. So Fabi bit back her hurt and left the lunch line.

She rushed over to her sister's table. Alexis was eating her lunch with a couple of her friends.

"Are you okay?" Alexis asked, sensing something was up.

Fabi tried to smile. "Yeah, it's cool."

"Aren't you going to eat?" Alexis motioned at the french fries, chili cheese dog, bag of cookies, and soda on her tray. Fabi had left her lunch tray at the counter.

"I lost my appetite."

"Hey." Milo joined them, holding two lunch trays. "You left this," he said, offering her the tray with green peas and milk. Milo was so considerate, she thought, looking at the food he got for her.

"What happened?" Alexis demanded. She glanced back at the line and noticed Melodee with her gang.

"It was nothing." Fabi just wanted to end the conversation.

"Don't let her get under your skin," Alexis said, trying to sound braver than she actually was. "Melodee is a psycho loser who is just jealous because she has zero personality. The only reason she has friends is because they're all scared of her." Alexis had experienced Melodee's wrath firsthand when she dated Dex — who was Melodee's ex-boyfriend.

Fabi sighed heavily. "You're right. She's not even that pretty up close, you know? With that little beak nose of hers that she always has in the air like she smells caca or something, and those beady eyes all smudged over with charcoal eye shadow like a raccoon!"

"Totally!" Alexis laughed.

Trash-talking about Melodee felt good. Melodee thought she was so tough, but she was just a bully. "You should have heard her in the lunch line," Fabi said, nodding to Milo for confirmation. "She was all talking about her quinceañera, how big it's going to be, how much of her parents' money she's going to spend. The girl is a serious poseur. She's not even Mexican!"

A coughing sound made Fabi look over her shoulder. Her breath caught and she swallowed. Melodee Stanton was standing right behind her. Melodee's pulled-back blonde hair and smoky eye shadow made her piercing gray eyes look especially evil. Fabi wanted to curl into a ball and roll away. Melodee was making a big foul face. Her lunch tray was pressed against her hip. The chatter in the lunchroom died down to an eerie silence. Everyone stopped to listen.

"So, Fatty apparently does have a spine after all," Melodee said.

Fabi looked around, feeling the heat rise to her cheeks.

"What? Don't look away. You were talking smack behind my back. Now what? You've lost your tongue? You got something to tell me? Tell it to my face."

"Ah, I'm sorry," Fabi began, getting up to explain that it was all just a joke.

"You're sorry? I'm the one who's sorry. I'm sorry for saving your sorry-ass cousin. This is the thanks I get. Forget you're *sorry*."

Melodee pushed the tray into Fabi, trying to rile her up.

Alexis scurried around the table. "Get your stinky hands off my sister," she cried.

Melodee laughed. "Oh, how cute," she said to her crew. "Little sister has to stick up for poor Fatty."

One of Melodee's crew cheered, "Yeah, Melodee, you tell her."

"Oh, shut up!" Alexis snapped.

"Alexis, stop," Fabi said, trying to keep her sister out of it. "Milo, help me," she said as she pulled her sister away. But she also knew Alexis had just as much right to be mad at Melodee.

Melodee sneered. "Yeah, Milo, hold back your loser girlfriend's sister before she gets hurt." She turned back to Fabi. "So when did you become Ms. Quinceañera Expert, huh?" Her friends chuckled at Melodee's joke. "Oh, wait, I forgot. You're already fifteen and didn't have a quinceañera. Couldn't afford it, could you? It must suck to be poor."

"That's not true!" cried Alexis.

"Oh, no," Melodee said, pressing her pinky

fingertip to her mouth in a fake surprised expression.

"Alexis —" Fabi had to try to defuse the situation that Alexis was making worse. She couldn't care less about quinceañeras. She just had to get out of there.

"For your information, Fabi is having a quinceañera," Milo stated. Fabi felt like she was going to choke.

"Yeah!" Alexis agreed. "And it's going to be the biggest *pachanga* ever."

Melodee looked Fabi up and down and rolled her eyes. "Yeah, right."

"It is," Milo exclaimed. "We got the hottest band."

"Yeah, who?" Melodee snapped. She shook her head. "No, my quinceañera is going to be the biggest party in the Valley."

"Oh, really?" Alexis said. "Well, we're just going to have to see about that. All I know is, we turned down the convention center because it was too small."

"Guys," Fabi hissed between clenched teeth.

"Too small?" Melodee began to laugh, but then stopped. She stared Fabi in the eyes, as if trying to drill a hole to the truth. "All right," she said with a nod. "You think your quince will be better than mine? It's on. You and me." She pointed to Fabi. "We'll have a quinceañera competition. And everyone here will vote."

Melodee turned to talk to the crowd. "You got that, everyone? You're all invited and you will vote for the best quinceañera. The loser has to —"

Fabi gulped.

"Shave her head," Milo suggested. Fabi elbowed him to shut up.

"Be the winner's servant for a week," Alexis said.

"Hey," Santiago called out from behind them. *When did he get here?* Fabi wondered. "Why not do both? Bald chicks are hot." He gave Fabi a wink.

"Guys." Fabi rolled her eyes and slapped her sister on the arm. "You're not helping."

Melodee smiled wickedly. It made Fabi cringe like there were hundreds of spiders crawling up her body. "The loser," Melodee stated loud enough for everyone to hear, "must be a *bald slave* for a *whole week* and do whatever the winner says." Melodee turned her devilish grin right at Fabi and declared, "This is going to be the best quinceañera battle in history. I hope you're ready."

Fabi felt the blood drain from her face. She never wanted a quinceañera in the first place. Now she had to have one — and not just any quinceañera. Fabi had to have the biggest, best quince the Valley had ever seen.

Looking around the cafeteria at the sea of bobbing faces, Fabi started to feel queasy. She wasn't sure if she was going to faint or barf.

chapter 3

The mood was upbeat and festive when Fabi pushed open the doors of her family's restaurant. The music of Little Rafa, Fabi's late grandfather and a Tex-Mex icon, was playing on the jukebox. Her mother, Magda, was yelling an order for carne asada over the music and the noisy chatter of customers filling the tables. Fabi closed her eyes and took in a deep breath.

The familiar scent of rice and beans enveloped her like a warm embrace from an old friend. Garza's was her first childhood memory. She remembered running into the kitchen and latching on to her father's leg as he tried to cook. He would pretend not to notice and then say, "And where did this little monkey come from?" That's how she got her nickname "*changuita*," little monkey. But it had been years since anyone called her that. Now, as a young woman of fifteen years, everyone called her Fabi, short for Fabiola.

For a split second, Fabi actually felt like everything would be all right. But then reality came crashing in behind her. Alexis burst through the front door with Milo at her heels.

"Okay," Alexis stated, throwing her arms in the air like a traffic guard. "I don't want you to worry about a thing. I already have it all figured out."

"No," Fabi protested, "you two have done enough." She tucked her books under the counter and grabbed an apron. "Maybe I can reason with Melodee — if you guys just stop *helping*." Fabi hurried over to her mother, who was busy clearing a table of plates, cups, utensils, and used napkins. Her parents worked really hard every day and it tugged at her heart to see them so stressed all the time. "Sorry, Mom. We got here as fast as we could. Milo's car broke down a block away and we had to push it."

Magda made a forget-about-it gesture with her hand. Her mom was old-school and always wore dresses, stockings, and small black pumps. Fabi's dad, Leonardo, was a towering figure with thick wavy hair. He paused on his way to the refrigerated room to cough, before pulling the heavy door. Her parents were very different from her, and sometimes they didn't all understand one another.

"No worries," her mother said. "I had a surprise assistant."

"Really?" Fabi looked around the restaurant with an inquisitive expression. Lydia and Lorena, the waitress staff, were busy at their stations — which was a surprise. Those two were always calling in late or sick.

But everything else looked normal. Grandma Trini was feeding Fabi's two-year-old baby brother mashed-up beans. Grandfather Frank was in his usual seat. A circle of old retired war vets was standing around him, swapping stories. On the other side of the restaurant sat her other grandmother, Abuela Alpha Omega, as always.

Just then a guy came out from the kitchen with a tray. She didn't recognize him at first in his hairnet and long white apron. Then it hit her like a sack of beans. It was Santiago — and he was bussing tables! Fabi rubbed her eyes to make sure she was seeing correctly. Something was definitely not right. First Santiago went to school on time, and then he came to the restaurant to help? It had to be a sign of the end of days.

"When did Santiago get here?" Fabi asked.

Magda smiled. "I know. I can barely believe it myself. I had to take a picture with my phone and send it to his mom. He got here about an hour ago and just started doing whatever needed to get done." She put her hand on Fabi's. "Why don't you just start on your homework? I think we've got enough help."

"Really?" Fabi didn't know how to feel. She always worked after school.

"I don't know how long this is going to last, so you might as well take advantage."

Fabi smiled and balled up her apron. She turned, not quite sure what to do with all this time she'd been granted.

Then she spotted Alexis. Her sister was supposed to be practicing her violin scales, but Alexis and Milo had gathered Grandma Trini and Abuelita Alpha to a table by the jukebox. Fabi did *not* like the excitement on her sister's face. Was her sister already making this quinceañera business even worse?

Walking up to their table, Fabi's suspicions were confirmed.

"Oh, you should have seen that Melodee," Alexis was telling their grandmothers. "I thought she was going to faint when I told her the convention center was too small for Fabi's quince."

"But it is," exclaimed Grandma Trini. "Much too small for my *guapa*." She turned to Fabi and pinched her cheek excitedly, pulling her closer to the table.

Abuelita Alpha motioned for Fabi to sit next to her. Her tight white hair bun, black clothes, and pale face contrasted with Grandma Trini, who was always fighting age spots and wrinkles with beauty creams, makeup, and chemical peels.

"Now, Fabi," Alpha began, looking at her sideways. "I'm glad to hear that you've finally come to your senses and are ready to affirm your dedication to the church. You know, it's really short notice, but I think that if you promise to fast for fourteen days, Father Benavides may overlook your lack of enthusiasm for Bible camp and squeeze you in for the next open quinceañera service."

"What? No." Fabi shook her head. "I am not having a quinceañera. I'm going to New York City."

"Oh, no you're not," Alexis cut in. "Remember, Dad said you weren't responsible enough to go away by yourself."

"Yeah, well, he could change his mind, you know? And I only got in trouble because you snuck out of the house to go to that party."

"No, it was God's will," Abuelita Alpha interrupted.

"Everyone just stop," Fabi stated. "Milo, tell them. Tell them this whole quinceañera business is all a mistake. You spoke out of turn. You didn't really mean it."

They all turned to Milo, who had up until then been as quiet as a stone. But instead of explaining what happened in the cafeteria, he said, "Why don't you want a quinceañera? It'll be so much fun. I went to a couple in Phoenix and all the girls seem to love it. The big dresses, the cake, the dancing. I can be your *chambelán* —"

"I can't believe I'm even having this conversation! Do I look like *all the girls* to you?" Fabi blushed. "Wait. Don't answer that. I mean I'm not like other girls. I don't want a party. I want to go to New York. I want to get out of this town!"

Her grandmothers flinched.

"I mean," Fabi tried to backpedal. "Look, we don't even have the money for a quinceañera. I have five hundred saved in the bank that I got from my birthday, but that's not enough. Melodee is renting the McAllen Convention Center. Do you even know how much that place costs? She's having her dress made by some fancy designer in Austin. And she's probably going to hire some famous singer to be there. I can't compete with that. I don't *want* to."

"God does not care where you have your quinceañera," Alpha said.

"Yeah, but everyone at school does," Fabi tried to explain. "And now, thanks to Alexis and Milo, I'll have to shave my head and be Melodee's slave for a week."

Abuelita Alpha got up, shaking her head. "I don't understand you kids. You don't want a quinceañera," she said, pointing to Fabi. "And you two" — she gestured at Alexis and Milo — "are making up tales you know aren't true, *pa' qué?*"

"Because Melodee is a brat and someone has to stand up to her," Alexis stated heatedly.

"Then why don't *you* stand up to her?" Alpha suggested.

Alexis blushed and looked away.

"*Ya*, Alpha," Grandma Trini interrupted. "*Pobres huercos* are just trying to help. They need understanding, not your scolding. Besides, *no hay quinceañera fea.*"

Abuelita Alpha nodded and she sat back down. Trini was right. There was no such thing as a bad quinceañera.

Grandma Trini turned to Fabi and cupped her hands over her granddaughter's. "Now, *mija*, I know this is not what you had in mind for your birthday celebration, but you need to stop thinking about yourself for one *minuto*, okay?"

Fabi nodded, feeling a bit confused. She wasn't sure if it was from all the excitement, the quick movement from her grandmother's glittery false lashes, or the heavy scent of her Jean Naté perfume. But she listened as her grandmother went on.

"You have to think of *la familia*. We Garzas have a reputation to uphold."

"She's only half Garza!" interrupted Abuelita Alpha. "The other half is Ibarra. That's Basque, you know," she said to Milo. "From Spain."

Grandma Trini cleared her throat pointedly. "Like I was saying. You are a Garza. You're the granddaughter of the one and only Tejano Hall of Famer Little Rafa 'Los Dedos del Valle' Treviño Garza — don't you forget that. And more important, you have my hair. There is no way," she said, shaking a long manicured nail in Fabi's face, "*no* way that I will let you shave your beautiful head."

Her grandmother pulled Fabi into a tight embrace, petting Fabi's hair lovingly. Fabi wanted to cry out in frustration, but she couldn't breathe because her grandmother was pressing her head down to her chest. What was she going to do?

When her grandmother finally released her for some air, Fabi noticed that Santiago was getting along really well with the customers and even her dad was smiling from the kitchen.

This could not last, she told herself. Milo smiled brightly at her from across the table.

"What's your problem?" she asked him.

"Your family. They're great. My parents don't even talk to each other. All they do is watch TV and drink. But your relatives are just so passionate about everything."

"You want them?" Fabi motioned to her grandma Trini, who was adjusting her brassiere as if she was in her home alone. "You can have all of them."

Milo laughed.

"You like the older ladies, don't you, *mijo*?" Grandma Trini asked Milo, smiling seductively. "You know that show *Cougar Town*? I like that show. I want a show like that one but for women my age."

"Grandma!" Fabi and Alexis cried together.

"*Ay, Diosito.*" Abuelita Alpha pulled her rosary from her bosom. "Please take this lost soul," she said, referring to Grandma Trini. "Take her now."

"*Ay*, Alpha." Trini slapped Abuelita Alpha's thigh. "I was just teasing the *muchacho*. I know he's just a baby. You need to relax. If you just let your hair down." She reached for Abuelita

Alpha's hair tie. "You remember when you used to wear your hair loose? We used to have fun, didn't we?"

"Have you no shame?" Alpha cried, getting up.

Grandma Trini started to crack up as the other *abuelita* stormed back to her side of the restaurant. "Don't you worry about her," Trini said to Alexis, Fabi, and Milo. "She's all big hat, no cattle. Now, Fabi," she said, growing serious. "Have you talked to your parents about this? I'm sure that now that you're not going to New York they'll be more willing to help you out for your quinceañera."

"Well, I haven't —" Fabi began and stopped. When had she crossed that point of no return? So now she *was* having a quinceañera? Fabi sighed. There was just no fighting the family.

"Go, talk to your mother right now," Trini said, pushing Fabi forward. "See, she's all alone looking at that book. It's a perfect opportunity. I know she's going to be so *thrilliada*. I know I am!"

Her mother would *not* be thrilled, Fabi thought as she got up. Magda was leaning over the register counter, which also held gum, candies, postcards, and other trinkets. She was reviewing the bankbooks, adding up sums with her small calculator. Fabi thought about turning back. But Alexis, Grandma Trini, and Milo had their heads huddled together, watching her every move.

"Hey, Mom," Fabi said as she approached.

Magda raised a finger in the air for Fabi to wait. Fabi noticed the pile of letters to her mother's right. They were overdue hospital bills. Fabi's dad had been recently diagnosed with type 2 diabetes. There were lots of tests and doctor visits now. Visits and tests that their health insurance would not cover, so they had to pay out of pocket. Fabi wasn't supposed to be concerned, but how could she not be, when she heard her parents arguing at night about the bills, when they thought the kids were asleep?

"It's nothing." Fabi turned to leave.

"No, it's fine," Magda said, removing her reading glasses. "What is it?"

Fabi pressed her lips together. What was she thinking? Her family couldn't throw her a quinceañera. Even if they didn't have the hospital bills, her parents still struggled. Fabi went without braces so that her sister could get voice lessons once a week. The quinceañera was an unnecessary expense.

Magda smiled at Fabi, encouraging her to go on.

Just then Alexis came up behind Fabi. "We got it! We got it all figured out. Did she tell you, Mom?" Alexis asked her mother.

"Tell me what?" she asked, sensing Alexis's enthusiasm.

"About Fabi's quinceañera!"

"What? Oh, my!" her mother exclaimed. Fabi noticed with surprise the sudden twinkle in her mother's eyes. "What are you talking about? When did this happen? *Mija* —" She turned to Fabi. Her eyes were dancing with hope. "I thought you didn't —"

"It just happened, Mom," Alexis gushed. "Isn't it wonderful? I'm so excited." Alexis hugged their mom and then pulled Fabi in with her other arm. Once again, Alexis was oblivious to Fabi's lack of enthusiasm.

"This is so wonderful," Magda said, tears forming in her eyes. "I had given up hope when you said you wanted to go to New York. But this —" She clapped her hands together. "This is the best news." She turned to Alexis. "We have to start planning right away. It won't be a big one, of course, but I'm sure we can do something real nice at the park. Maybe your grandpa will butcher a goat? Oh." She noted Fabi's stunned expression. "Don't worry, *mija*. We will take care of everything. All you'll have to do is show up."

"But, Mom." Fabi had to jump in. "I don't want anything too big, okay? I know we have a lot of bills with Dad being sick."

Alexis had started to bounce excitedly. "But that's what I was trying to tell you. We got it all figured out. Look." She pointed to the small TV by the gumdrop machine.

Fabi, her mother, and Alexis moved closer to the TV. Grandma Trini and Milo were viewing the show with the utmost attention. They were watching a girl around Fabi's age in crutches, waltzing around the dance floor with an older man in a military uniform.

"See that girl?" Grandma Trini motioned to the screen. Her grandmother looked up with red teary eyes. "She was in a car bomb as a baby and lost her leg. She never knew her father and they just found him. He was in Iraq, a military man. The girl's quinceañera dream was to be reunited with her biological father for the father-daughter dance." Trini grabbed one of the crocheted handkerchiefs she was selling and blew her nose. "Isn't that just beautiful?"

Fabi noticed Milo scribbling in his notebook. "What is going on here?" she asked, growing suspicious.

Grandma Trini slapped Fabi's hand playfully. "Taking notes, *mensa*."

"See, Mom," Alexis explained. "It's a new reality TV show called *Quince Dreams*. If we get selected, they'll pay for everything: the dress, the hall, the *recuerdos*, everything. It'll be perfect. All we need is to write a really good story."

"I don't think anyone is going to want to come to the Rio Grande Valley," Fabi stated flatly. "Plus, my life is super boring. No one is going to want to watch it."

"Oh, come on," Alexis insisted. "They have to come. Imagine Melodee's face when she finds out that your quinceañera will be on TV."

Fabi smiled and admitted, "That would be nice. But how are you —"

"Leave that up to us!" Grandma Trini said, sweeping one arm into the air with flair.

Fabi's chest started to tighten. Things were spinning *way* out of control. She could feel herself standing at the mercy of the incoming family storm. Her eyes darted to her friend, her sister, her *abuelita* — anyone who might rescue her. But no one seemed to notice or dared to come between Fabi and her quinceañera.

chapter 4

Santiago was now a regular student, doing homework and working at the restaurant after school. Fabi didn't understand the change, but she was too busy hiding from quince talk to find out. Melodee's cold stare seemed to be everywhere — by her locker, in the bathroom mirror, even in the hallway bulletin. A big photo of her as the student who sold the most chocolates at the school fund drive seemed to be on every surface. *Big deal*, Fabi thought. She'd probably bought them all herself.

Everyone at school was talking about the big showdown.

But there had been no word from the *Quince Dreams* show, and Fabi was somewhat relieved. For a second there, she actually believed that her family might be able to pull it off. Winning the bet with Melodee was the real quince dream. She didn't know how she would face her. Now, no matter how much she cried and begged, Fabi would have to go through with having a quinceañera. The word was out. Abuelita Alpha had invited Father Benavides to the restaurant to talk to Fabi over a plate of migas. There was no going back. Fabi was going to have a quinceañera, big or small, whether she liked it or not.

That Saturday, Fabi met up with her best friend, Georgia Rae, at the mall. It had been weeks since they'd hung out. When Georgia Rae first moved away to McAllen at the beginning of the school year, they'd promised to see each other every weekend. But now that Fabi's BFF was starring in a major school play, she spent all her free time rehearsing or hanging out with her new artsy friends. Fabi couldn't help but feel left behind. They didn't talk about it, but the distance between them was starting to get on both of their nerves.

Fabi admired a party dress on an anorexic-looking mannequin in a display window. She never really bought anything at the mall;

she just liked to window-shop and people-watch. The mall was the second-best place to go to beat the heat — the movies was number one. Georgia Rae said nothing, glaring into the distance. Fabi could tell she was fuming on the inside.

"I can't believe you caved in just like that. You have to say no once in a while," Georgia Rae said as they walked past a shoe store.

"I didn't get a chance. You know my family. They just took over like they always do. This quince is being shoved down my throat. I'm not even a part of it. My mom seriously told me just to show up."

Georgia Rae stopped in front of a bookstore and stared inside, thinking. Finally, she turned back to Fabi and said, "I don't know. Your family always seems to get in the way, and you always just let them. I just don't get it. That was your money. You should be able to do whatever you want with it."

"But it wasn't even like that," Fabi tried to explain. "Melodee started it —" Georgia Rae huffed in annoyance and glanced away. Fabi could tell she was tired of hearing about Melodee Stanton, Dos Rios, and anything that had to do with that small town. Fabi followed her friend's eyes to a group of artsy teenagers. They were laughing loudly and eating fries together on a raised platform. Fabi worried, for the millionth time, if now that her best friend was at a new school, Georgia Rae would forget all about her. "I'm sorry," Fabi said. "I know we planned to go to New York."

"Yeah. We were supposed to see a big Broadway show."

"And we still will," Fabi said, trying to sound hopeful.

"When?" Georgia Rae asked.

Fabi shrugged. "I don't know. We'll figure it out, okay?" It was obvious that something was bugging her best friend, but she was not coming out with it. "Hey, you want some pizza?" Georgia Rae just shrugged.

Fabi headed to the pizza stand in the food court. Lots of teenagers worked at the mall. It was a highly prized job if you could get it. Her sister, Alexis, was dying to work at the mall. Fabi ordered two slices of vegetarian pizza.

The boy behind the counter smiled. "You like vegetarian? Hardly anyone orders that."

Fabi looked sideways at Georgia Rae and gave him a quick smile. She shoved a bill at him.

The boy continued talking as if they were old friends. "I don't know why more people don't order it. It's real good. It's my favorite, actually. Oh, yeah," he said, taking Fabi's money. "Okay, here's your change. I can bring it to you, if you like?"

Fabi nodded and quickly turned to find an empty table. She was sure that her face had to be bright pink. Georgia Rae poked her softly as they walked away.

"That boy was sooooooooo trying to talk to you."

Fabi's heartbeat began to race. "No." She shook her head. "He was just being nice. That's his job."

Georgia Rae's face lit up. "Yeah, right! He offered to bring our food. C'mon, don't tell me that's regular customer service."

Fabi's chest tightened. Was Georgia Rae right? Was he flirting? Fabi quickly glanced over her shoulder. The boy was handling the order of another customer. He was very cute, with short hair, a nice tan, and straight teeth. No. She shook her head. He was not flirting with her. Boys didn't flirt with her. Fabi had a bunch of guy friends. But they were just friends. Georgia Rae was trying to see things that weren't there.

A few minutes later, Georgia Rae grabbed her wrist and said, "Don't turn around," in an excited whisper.

Fabi felt trapped. She wanted to get out of there. But the pizza guy was standing next to her. There was nowhere for her to go without knocking him down, and that would be really hard to explain.

"Hey," he said, looking at Fabi. His big eyes pierced her like an arrow to her heart. She turned away, feeling her face getting red.

Thankfully, Georgia Rae jumped in. She reached for the plates. "Thank you so much. Would you like to join us?"

Fabi kicked Georgia Rae under the table. How could she be so bold? Georgia Rae winked at Fabi.

The guy didn't notice — he just smiled. He had a brilliant smile that lit up the entire food court and made Fabi's heart flutter. "I can't," he said, sounding really sorry. It made Fabi feel dizzy. "I already had my break. Let me know what you guys think, though. I made it up myself. Like I said, we don't usually get orders for vegetarian stuff."

"Well, thanks," Georgia Rae said. She raised her eyebrows at Fabi, but Fabi still couldn't speak.

"Oh," the guy added, smiling and looking embarrassed now, "my name's Daniel." He reached out his hand, but jerked back and wiped it on his pant leg before offering it again to Fabi.

"Hi," Fabi said, forgetting to say her name.

"You're Fabiola Garza, right?"

Fabi glanced at Georgia Rae, who seemed impressed. Georgia Rae kicked her under the table.

"Yup, that's me," Fabi replied, not knowing what else to say. This had to be the weirdest conversation ever. Who was this cute stranger? And how come he knew her name? "Do I know you?"

"We've never actually met. I know your cousin Santiago. We used to play together, baseball."

"Oh," Fabi said, feeling Georgia Rae's smirk. "I'm sorry. It's been so long since Santiago played."

"Yeah, I know. I went to his trial, but they didn't let me speak, there were so many people. I guess your cousin is pretty popular."

Fabi nodded. She couldn't stop smiling. He was so cute, with gorgeous dimples and warm eyes that made you want to melt.

Daniel glanced over his shoulder. There were a couple of people waiting for him at the stand. "I got to go," he said, licking his soft full lips as if trying to think of something else to say. "I'll see you around."

"Yeah," Fabi replied. As soon as he walked away, Fabi dropped her head onto the table. "Oh, my God. Did you just see that? Tell me I wasn't dreaming."

Georgia Rae looked like she wanted to jump out of her chair and shout. "You definitely weren't dreaming, girl! I told you he was trying to talk to you. He is so cute."

"Something has to be wrong with him," Fabi said, biting into the pizza. "Things like that don't happen. They don't happen to me."

"What? A cute boy can't talk to you? C'mon. You don't give yourself any credit. Why can't a boy like you?"

"Um, let's be honest. I've *never* been the girl

boys ask out. I'm the friend. And I'm cool with that. Besides, I don't want to date anyone here anyway. It'll just make things more complicated when I move away for college."

Georgia Rae tilted her head as if she hadn't heard Fabi correctly. "Now you're just talking stupid," she said, reaching for Fabi's hand and shaking it a little. "Get real. A cute boy wants to talk to you. That's it. We're not talking marriage, just the possibility of something. Don't fight it or try to figure it out. Just *enjoy it*."

Fabi took a deep breath. She glanced over her shoulder to make sure Daniel was still there and hadn't turned into a troll or anything like that. He was lifting up a pie into the big pizza oven. Fabi noticed a drop of sweat rolling down the right side of his face. It made Fabi feel weak. What was happening to her? She turned back to her friend, who was staring excitedly back at her. "Take that smile off your face," Fabi snapped, pretending to be upset.

"What smile?" Georgia Rae teased, chewing with her mouth open.

Fabi shot her an evil look.

Georgia Rae burst out laughing. "Fine. I get it. Let's eat."

"Pizza!" a voice called out from behind them. A small hand appeared and snatched Fabi's slice off her plate. Milo smiled as he took a big bite of her lunch.

"Hey, go get your own!" Fabi said, snatching the slice out of his hand. Georgia Rae laughed. "Animal. That's what you are."

"Why didn't you tell me you were coming to the mall?" Milo asked, pretending to be hurt as he chewed. "I would have caught a ride."

"This is a girl's day," Georgia Rae stated. "And you are not a girl."

"Ah, c'mon. I can totally be a girl," he said, tossing his long bangs back with dramatic flair. "I love girl-bashing, too. Look at that hoochie's clothes." He motioned to a group of girls seated two tables down. "What was she thinking when she got dressed this morning?"

"Ha!" Georgia Rae laughed. "Yeah, but we're picking up guys, and we can't pick up guys with you standing right here."

"Why not?" Milo asked innocently. "What you two don't understand is the male psychology." Fabi and Georgia Rae gave him their full attention. "Men like a challenge. Boys see you with me and they think, 'Wow, those girls are hanging out with him. They must be cool.'"

Fabi couldn't help but start to crack up. "You are a fool."

"And we were actually doing fine before you got here," Georgia Rae said. "Isn't that right, Fabi?"

Fabi blushed. She didn't know why. Milo was their friend. But they never talked about boys around him. It felt strange.

"Oh, yeah?" Milo turned to Fabi. "Who you picking up?"

Georgia Rae leaned over the table. "See that hottie selling pizza?"

"The one picking his nose?" Milo asked.

"What?" Fabi and Georgia Rae cried out, turning to see.

Milo started to laugh. "I'm kidding." He looked at Daniel. "I guess his back is cute."

"You're crazy," Georgia Rae said. "He's gorgeous, and he's all into Fabi."

"I guess." He shrugged. "If you're into that tall, dark, and handsome look. I prefer guys who come in small packages with big personalities."

Georgia Rae rolled her eyes.

"Anyway, I just stopped to pick up a cable at Radio Shack," Milo said. "I didn't mean to bother your man hunt."

"We are not hunting," Fabi said. "We actually just came to the mall to get out of the heat."

Milo winked. "Right."

"Really."

He stood, stretching up to appear taller, and glanced around. "Well, it's getting too hot and heavy for me here. See you around."

Fabi watched Milo walk away. Why was he acting all weird? She turned to Georgia Rae with a frown. "What was that all about?"

Georgia Rae shrugged. "Who knows? Boys. Can't live with them. Can't kill them."

Fabi laughed, returning to what was left of her pizza.

chapter 5

Fabi tried to forget the quinceañera mess, including how upset it was making Georgia Rae. Luckily, she had plenty of schoolwork and things to do around the restaurant to keep her distracted. There was never enough time after school to do all her reading, so she started spending her lunch period in the library. It was well air-conditioned, and she was guaranteed not to bump into Melodee and her pack. Plus, Fabi liked to sit in the cubicles. It was private and there was plenty of space to spread out. Studying like this made her feel smarter, like a college student.

She was just starting to lose herself in her book when someone snuck up behind her and said, "So *this* is why we never run into each other."

Fabi turned and almost jumped out of her seat. It was the cute boy from the mall, the pizza boy, Daniel.

"Oh, hi!" she said, feeling her cheeks flush as her heartbeat pounded loudly in her ears like a drum. She casually wiped her sweaty palms on the edge of the plastic seat. She hoped he didn't notice.

Daniel smiled in a friendly manner as he leaned against the divider. He looked even better without the pizza uniform, Fabi thought, admiring his arms.

"Yeah . . ." Fabi tried to think of something smart or cool or funny to say. She was drawing a complete blank. "I like to read."

Daniel chuckled. "Me, too," he said, and raised a finger to his soft pouty lips in a "shh" gesture. "But don't tell anyone." He smiled again. "Mrs. Perales —" He motioned to the school librarian. "She picks out books she thinks I'll like and leaves them in the first cubby. She's great. She even takes off the book jackets so no one knows what kind of books I'm reading."

"Really?" Fabi couldn't help but be curious. "Like what kind of books? Romance?"

"No!" He laughed again. "I mean, I do like romance," he said, then suddenly blushed, his mouth dropping open in shock. "Wow, did I just say that out loud?"

Mrs. Perales looked up from her desk on the other side of the room and made a shushing sound at them, but in a nice way.

Daniel mouthed the word "sorry" to the librarian. Then he grabbed a chair and sat next to Fabi. Her heart started to thump. She couldn't believe this was actually happening. A cute boy was talking to her. His body was so close she could breathe him in. He smelled like peppermint candy. She would never smell peppermint candy again without thinking of him.

"Okay, so you promise not to laugh?" he said softly, snapping her out of her trance.

"Yes, I promise." Fabi would have promised him the moon, the stars, and the sun just to keep him talking.

He licked his lips slowly, glancing around to make sure no one was eavesdropping. "I kinda like fantasy books."

"Like *The Lord of the Rings*?"

"Yeah," he said, and sighed in relief. "Anything with magical animals and faeries. Stupid, huh?"

Fabi shook her head. "That's not stupid at all. I think it's kind of cool."

"You do?"

"Yeah, sure."

"You think I'm a nerd, huh?"

"No, I think you're . . . intriguing." She was secretly happy to finally get the chance to use this line.

Daniel leaned in close. "I think you're intriguing, too."

Fabi jerked back, feeling incredibly uncomfortable. Daniel was all around her: his chest, his nose — and those lips. She needed air. The cubicle was becoming unbearably stuffy. Just then the lunch bell rang. *Saved by the bell!* Fabi thought. She sprang out of her seat and whispered, "See you later," before bolting toward the door.

By the time she reached the hallway, her heart was racing and she suddenly became very confused. Which class did she have after lunch? Fabi raced for the first girls' bathroom and went into the last stall, locking the door behind her. She needed a minute to collect her thoughts, to get her head on straight. What was it about that boy Daniel that made her so frazzled? Fabi hated not being in control of her emotions, and this boy was making her *loca en la cabeza*.

If this is love, Fabi thought, *then maybe I can't handle it.*

Ahhh, did I just use the "L" word?!? She didn't even know Daniel's last name!

"Knock, knock!" an overly cheerful voice sang out, interrupting her thoughts.

Fabi peeked under the door and noticed a pair of suede animal-print flats. Fabi said meekly, "I'm busy."

"Now, I know you haven't been hiding from me," Melodee began, ignoring the fact that Fabi was standing in front of the toilet. "I seem to remember someone saying they were going to have a quinceañera. But the funny thing is, I haven't received my invitation. Strange, huh?"

This was the last thing Fabi needed. She was secretly hoping Melodee would forget about their bet. But now she seemed to be trapped. How would she get out of the stall without colliding with the girl? Fabi prayed someone, anyone, would walk in and rescue her. Where were the hall monitors when you needed them? But class had already started and Fabi was going to be marked absent. There was no escape. She flushed the empty toilet and walked out.

Melodee Stanton stood smiling in her pink tank and short skirt that accentuated her long legs. "So . . ." Melodee placed her hands on her hips, waiting.

"So, what?"

Melodee dropped her fake smile. "Where's my invitation, stupid?"

"Um . . . they're getting made." Fabi fumbled over her words. She had to get this girl off her back.

"Fine," Melodee huffed. She reached into her Gucci purse and pulled out a small pink envelope. "Well, here's an invitation to *my* party. You better not do yours on the same day, got it?"

Fabi took the invitation. She noticed that her name wasn't on the envelope, as if it was an extra. Melodee turned to leave. Her flats snapped loudly as she walked away. Fabi sighed in relief, releasing the breath she hadn't realized she'd been holding.

All of a sudden, Melodee spun around to face Fabi. "And if I can ask," she said in a suspiciously sweet voice, "who's going to be your *chambelán*?"

Fabi jerked. She wasn't expecting that.

"Your *date*?" Melodee prompted, rolling her eyes.

"I know what a *chambelán* is," Fabi snapped, trying to think quickly while acting cool — not an easy thing to do under Melodee Stanton's critical stare.

Melodee began to chuckle. "Don't tell me you're going to ask that shrimp, DJ Meko."

"His name is Hermilo," Fabi corrected. "And no, I wasn't going to ask him."

Melodee smiled. "Good."

At that moment, Fabi hated Melodee. Hated her like dog poo on the bottom of her shoe. Who did she think she was, insulting Fabi's friends like that? "For your information, I'm not asking Milo because I *have* a date. And he's the hottest boy at school."

"Oh, really," Melodee said mockingly. "And who is this 'hottest boy at school'?"

"I guess you'll just have to wait and see, won't you."

Melodee turned to admire herself in the mirror. Fabi wanted to slap that grin off her face. "I can't wait," Melodee said, and then turned and left without another word.

Fabi stood there a moment, still furious, and now terrified, too. There was only one boy she could think of who would fit the bill. She had to ask Daniel to be her *chambelán*. He seemed nice enough, didn't he? Of course, they'd just met, and the *chambelán* was kind of an important role. Most girls asked their boyfriends to do it. But Fabi didn't have a boyfriend, and she couldn't have her cousin or Milo do it. Plus, Daniel was the one she wanted.

She just hoped he'd say yes.

After school, Fabi found Santiago outside the school building. He was standing with the known troublemakers Brandon and Travis Salinas. The tension between them was thick. Brandon was saying something and Santiago was frowning. Her cousin waved them away, and when they called back to him, he ignored them. Fabi wondered what that was about.

"Everything okay?" she asked when she'd caught up to him.

Santiago shrugged. "I'm cool." He shifted his heavy backpack to his other shoulder. Fabi couldn't believe that he was still going to his classes. She'd even heard a rumor that he had joined the Science Olympiads team, a science club that competed with other schools in science experiments. Fabi had a hard time believing that, but decided not to ask Santiago about it right then.

"Woo, it's stifling out here," she said instead, peeling back her shirt collar for ventilation. "Where's Alexis?" Fabi glanced around for her sister. Students were streaming out of the main doors. A line of SUVs and trucks was parked in front. Suddenly, she saw a hand waving wildly in her direction. Alexis was running toward her. There was a crazed, excited look on her face that made Fabi nervous. When her sister was super excited, something bad usually happened. She tried to shake off her nerves.

Alexis ran up to them and screamed, "We got it!" She pulled Fabi and Santiago into a tight hug. "I just got the call. Can you believe it? Fabi, you're going to be famous! It worked! They want to talk to Mom and Dad. They're coming. They're actually coming here to Dos Rios!"

Fabi looked at her cousin for some support. Santiago looked as confused as she felt.

"What are you talking about?" he asked Alexis, tossing his curly locks out of his face.

"*Quince Dreams*! *Quince Dreams*! You" — Alexis thrust her arms up and at Fabi for emphasis — "were chosen for their next episode. I just got the call. Ms. Allen even gave me detention. You're not supposed to answer your phone during Algebra, but whatever." She rolled her eyes. "When I saw the unfamiliar area code, I had to answer it. Can you *believe* it? I'm so excited. We have to tell Milo and Grandma Trini. They're going to be so happy!"

Fabi couldn't believe her ears. Was this for sure? The look on her sister's face said yes, it was. The reality of the situation started to sink in.

And despite herself, she smiled. *Maybe now I can actually compete with Melodee and even win the bet!*

A car honked and the three of them glanced up to see Melodee waving at them from her new chili-red Mustang convertible. It was an early birthday gift from her father — or so her tweet said. Melodee didn't even have a license.

Fabi's blood started to boil, but then she thought about the look on Melodee's face, green with envy like the wicked witch of Oz, when she heard the news of Fabi's party. Fabi pictured herself dancing in a fancy designer dress with some handsome guy. She couldn't believe that this could actually happen. This was going to be the best quinceañera of all time! Fabi smiled smugly as she watched the Mustang disappear in a stream of trucks and SUVs exiting the school parking lot. Adios, Melodee Stanton!

chapter 6

By the end of that week, two words were on everyone's lips: *Quince Dreams*. Many had never heard of the show before. But when they learned a TV crew was coming to Dos Rios, they all became instant fans. Everyone in town wanted to be a part of the action.

Fabi tried to continue her daily routine, but people kept showing up at the restaurant to "check in" with her. City council member Rey Garcia III stopped by to talk about his reelection campaign and ask for her support. He left a dozen flyers, signs, and buttons. Mrs. Sanchez from the bakery down the street stopped by every day. She offered different pieces of cake for Fabi to try. The local paper wanted to do an article on her. Fabi didn't know how to handle her new celebrity status. At least her parents were happy — business had never been better.

At school, it was out of control. People she knew casually were acting like she was their best friend. Her lunch table filled up with new faces wanting to know all about the show, and what she planned to wear, and how she was going to do her hair. Even her teachers started to act strange, letting her turn in assignments late and dropping comments like, "You know, I almost had a part in a movie." She couldn't even walk down the halls without a dozen people following at her heels. Thankfully, Alexis and Milo were always there to keep her grounded and the masses at arm's length.

But if this was the price of fame, Fabi thought, it was worth the pain. All she could think about was the look on Melodee's face when she saw Fabi walking with her "I won" crowd down the halls. It was priceless.

Still, everything had its limits. When Fabi couldn't even go to the bathroom in peace, she knew she needed a break.

The back of the library was still her sanctuary. She found her cubicle empty, relished the peaceful quiet, and opened a book she had been looking forward to reading. Fabi was starting to get into it when someone snuck up on her.

"I thought I'd find you here."

Fabi looked up and into the warm chocolate eyes of Daniel. She never did get his last name. Well, *this* was an interruption she'd happily take any day.

"Hey, you," she said, smiling.

"I was trying to talk to you earlier, but I couldn't get past your bodyguards," he joked, referring to Alexis and Milo.

Fabi laughed. "Yeah, it's been pretty crazy lately, with all this TV stuff."

"So how does it feel to be an instant star?"

She shrugged. "I'm still the same person."

Daniel smiled, revealing his adorable dimples. "I'm glad to hear that. Hey, so is your party all set? I know we kind of just met and all . . . but if there's anything I can, you know, do . . . to help you with your party . . . I do look pretty good in a tux, you know?"

Fabi's mouth dropped. An awkward silence passed between them.

Daniel's face reddened. He looked away shyly. "So . . . what are you reading?"

Fabi blushed and admitted, "My guilty pleasure." She held up a chick lit book. "There's no faeries, but it's set in New York and it's really cool."

He reached out for the book and read the back summary. "Maybe I can borrow it when you're done."

"Fabi!" Alexis stormed in like a category five hurricane. She paid no mind to the librarian shushing her from the other end of the room. Her sister stopped short when she noticed that Fabi was not alone.

Fabi waved her over. "Alexis, this is my friend Daniel . . . Daniel . . . ah . . ."

He extended his hand out to her sister. "Daniel Cruz."

Alexis gave Fabi a sly wink. "Very, *very* nice to meet you, Daniel. Fabi forgot to mention you." She shook her head at Fabi and crinkled her nose. "Sisters. But I guess there's been a lot of stuff going on lately that *you forgot*!"

"This is the library," the librarian said out loud, interrupting Alexis.

Alexis waved and mouthed the word "sorry," then turned back to Fabi. "They're here," she whispered loudly. "The *Quince*

Dreams people are here and they want to see you."

"Here? Now?"

Alexis nodded. She grabbed Fabi's arm and started to pull her toward the door.

"Sorry," Fabi said to Daniel. "Got to go."

Daniel folded his arms across his chest and said, "Don't worry about it. Catch you later."

"Why didn't you tell me you had a new 'friend'?" Alexis demanded as soon as they reached the hallway.

"I only just met him," Fabi explained. "It's nothing. We just talk about books."

"Books. Really? Now, why don't I believe you?" Alexis pinched her softly on the arm. "He's dreamy."

"I know." Fabi felt her face get hot. "But I'm sure it's nothing like that." Fabi thought about his offer to "help." Did he really mean it or was he just trying to get on TV?

Alexis stopped and turned to her sister. "And why not? You're beautiful."

Fabi dismissed Alexis's comment with her hand. "Whatever."

Alexis stopped walking and stared at her. "Oh, my God, Fabi's got a *boyfriend*," she teased.

"You take that back!" Fabi demanded. She could feel her cheeks flush, and raised a fist in Alexis's face. "You better not say that again if you plan to see another birthday."

Alexis laughed, ignoring Fabi's threat. "This is exactly why you need this show," she continued in a dreamy voice. There was a small smile creeping up her lips. "You don't know what a gem you are."

Fabi rolled her eyes.

"You are a princess, and now, through *Quince Dreams*, the whole world will see it," Alexis stated, raising one arm in the air with flair and taking a bow.

Fabi looked for the camera. That sounded way too rehearsed. When Fabi was sure that no one was around, she raised her finger in a threatening manner to her sister. "You better not say anything embarrassing like that on camera or I'll never speak to you again."

Alexis grinned back a bit too excitedly. Fabi prayed that her little sister wouldn't embarrass her.

She entered the principal's office. It was the first time that Fabi had been in there — she'd never gotten in trouble. Dr. Mick Hudson sat behind his desk. His walls were covered in awards and school pictures. He was a small man with hairy hands and a balding head who walked around the hallways scowling at everyone, but today he was all smiles.

"Miss Fabiola Garza," he said, getting up and waving her in. He was sitting across from an elegantly dressed, full-figured young woman with supershort dark hair. Fabi liked her immediately. A muscular guy with a cool goatee was standing by the window. He wore a Dodgers baseball cap backward and balanced a big camera on his shoulder. "I was just telling Mrs. —"

"It's Ms. Cooper. Ms. Grace Cooper." She extended her manicured hand to Fabi. "You can call me Grace."

Fabi extended her hand to Grace. The woman shook it firmly. Fabi made a note to herself that she had to shake people's hands firmly like Grace. It showed confidence and sass. Fabi smiled, feeling a bit starstruck. The woman was so polished and sophisticated. She looked like she'd just walked off a magazine cover. Grace smiled sweetly at Fabi.

"I'm the production manager for *Quince Dreams*. We're so excited to be here and to finally meet you. In these next couple of weeks, leading up to your big day, we plan to get some interviews and make sure everything is in order." She looked more closely at Fabi. "How are you feeling? I know this is a lot."

"Yeah, it's all so overwhelming. I can't believe you're actually here. So it's really going to happen?"

Grace reached out and gave her a squeeze. "Of course it is. Fabi, from this moment on, don't you worry about a thing. That's my job to make happen. You just sit back and let me handle everything."

Dr. Hudson coughed softly and said, "I'd like to get back to what I was saying about possible sponsorship."

Grace interrupted, "Sure, but first, can you tell me a bit about Fabiola?"

Dr. Hudson chuckled softly and glanced at Fabi. "Miss Garza is one of our most valued students." He winked. "She's such a role model to the young girls of the Valley — a real gem." Fabi stared at him in disbelief. He was starting to sound like her sister. "Why, I was just telling the staff that we needed to honor her in some way."

"I think that's a great idea." Grace took out a small notepad and started to scribble a note. "Maybe at the quinceañera, you can present an award to her?"

The principal laughed. "I was just thinking the same thing."

Fabi didn't understand what was going on. She watched the two adults plan her party as if they knew her. The principal had never said two words to her before today and now he wanted to give her an award. This was not what she expected. Fabi had to talk to her sister. She looked at the clock. Fifth period had started fifteen minutes ago. Maybe the principal would write her a note?

"Excuse me," Fabi said, trying to get their attention. "Um . . . Dr. Hudson . . . I think I need to go back to class. I don't want to get in trouble."

"Nonsense, Fabiola," he said, smiling brightly. "This is a very important event for Dos Rios High School. You only turn fifteen once."

"But I'm already fifteen," she informed him.

"A technicality. Please, have a seat." He motioned to an empty chair. "Do you want something to drink? Some soda, perhaps?"

Fabi shook her head, pressing her lips together. She did not like this turn of events one bit. Grace Cooper read the hesitation on her face.

"We can continue our interview later," she said to the principal, closing her notebook. With the flick of her wrist, she motioned to the cameraman to follow. "Right now I'd like to talk to Fabi, and maybe some of her teachers and friends."

Dr. Hudson spread his arms out wide. "Talk to whoever you like. Dos Rios High is honored to have you and your camera friend on our campus. Now, this show of yours, will it be televised nationally?"

"Coast to coast," Grace said as she led Fabi out of the office.

"You all come back anytime," Dr. Hudson said with a grin.

They walked down the hallway for a couple steps. The cameraman seemed to be having a hard time with the equipment, huffing loudly behind them.

"Is it always this hot around here?" Grace asked. Her voice was light and playful.

Fabi nodded, fanning herself with her hand. "April is pretty bad. But just be glad it's not July or August. That's when the *canícula* hits. They say you can fry an egg on the sidewalk. I've never tried it. My dad would throw a fit if I wasted an egg. Thank God for air-conditioning, although my *abuelita* Alpha doesn't care for the AC; she says it's not good for her lungs and refuses to get one for her house —" Fabi was babbling and caught herself.

Grace laughed politely. "Now, Fabi, you're a very special girl. I must tell you, we chose you over hundreds of other entries."

Fabi flinched. *Hundreds!*

"You're just the perfect girl for *Quince Dreams*. To be honest, I truly loved your story. I pushed really hard to get you selected. Now" — her voice dropped and her face became serious — "I don't want you to change for the camera. If you've seen our show, you'll know that some girls have been very dramatic, a bit over the top. They become very demanding, start fights with their friends, etc. We actually had a stabbing in the last show.

That's not what we're trying to do here. *Quince Dreams* is trying to change its image. Put more heartfelt stories on air. Showcase Latina role models who are making a difference in their communities."

Fabi tried to hold her smile even though anxiety was running loose throughout her body — out of control. She didn't know how to react to Grace's comment. Role model? Her? Where was Alexis? She should be here. Alexis and Grandma Trini submitted the entry to *Quince Dreams*. Who knew what they actually wrote. Worry started to fester in Fabi's stomach. But she couldn't say anything to Grace. Fabi couldn't ruin this opportunity. It was her only chance of winning the bet with Melodee. Plus, the whole town was now expecting the ultimate televised quince experience. One of Abuelita Alpha's sayings rang out in her mind: *"Al mal tiempo buena cara."* She put on a brave face and smiled despite her growing anxiety.

"I want you to pretend like the camera is not even there," Grace instructed. "We want some shots of you in class, at home, and at your job — doing normal stuff. I'd like to interview your best friends, the girls who're going to be your *damas*."

"Okay, that's easy."

Grace reviewed her notes and went on, "I think it's great that you asked your grandmother to be a *dama*. I've never heard of anyone doing that. But you two sound real close. Grandma . . ."

"Trinidad," Fabi said through clenched teeth. She was going to kill her grandmother when she got home. "That's me," Fabi said, harsher than she wanted to. "Good ol' Fabi."

Grace smiled. "Now, there're a couple of other things you need to know about our show. Our sponsors provide all the items for the party. They're amazing and we'll just need to do some product placement, nothing major. We'll weave it into the event. You won't even notice. We've got the runner-up on *America's Top Fashion Designer* to make the gowns. She'll be calling this week to set up fittings and talk themes and colors."

"Really!" Fabi loved that show.

"*Tarjay* will be providing all the decorations, mementos, tableware, dishware, everything you can imagine. They're even covering the choreographer for the dance. Who is" — she paused for emphasis — "none other than Jennifer Lopez's personal dance choreographer!"

"No way!" Fabi's worries faded as she grew more excited.

"And that's not all. We just signed on the hot new reggaeton dance hall duo from Guatemala, Los Duendes del Don. Have you heard of them? Anyway, they'll be releasing their latest single at your quinceañera. Oh, Fabi." Grace put her arm around Fabi's shoulders. Fabi couldn't believe her luck — she felt like a winning contestant on some game show. Grace sighed with another heartfelt smile. "This is going to be the best party of your life. I guarantee you."

Fabi couldn't believe her luck. Maybe her grandma Trini tricked her way into being a *dama*. But this show was going to save her family a ton of money, and she was going to have the most amazing party of all time. People would be talking about her quinceañera for years to come. This was really a quinceañera's dream come true.

"So . . . ?" Grace asked. They were standing in the main entrance. Fabi noticed that they were right on top of the mosaic of the fighting catfish — the school mascot. "There was no mention of a *chambelán* in your story. We were all wondering if there was a special someone you had in mind."

Fabi felt her cheeks grow hot.

"There is! I knew it. Who is he? Does he go to school here?"

Grace was so cool, Fabi thought. She was like the older sister she'd never had. Fabi felt like she could tell her anything.

"Well, there is this boy," Fabi began.

"Yes?"

She knew that her cheeks were turning bright red. But she forced herself to go on. "His name is Daniel Cruz."

"Have you asked him?"

"No."

"What are you waiting for? Fabi, I know we're kind of rushing you. We had to push forward the party to get it in for this season. I really think this may be the best show ever produced." Grace glanced at her thin watch and then smiled at Fabi again. "There's no time like the present."

•   •   •

They looked up Daniel's schedule in the office. The clerk, Mrs. Galvan, was more than eager to supply them with whatever information they needed. "He has PE in the gym for another twenty minutes," she said.

As they stood at the doorway of the gymnasium, Fabi paused. She couldn't believe she was actually doing this. But Grace had this superwoman confidence that was rubbing off on Fabi. It made her feel like she was actually in control of her life. Plus, she didn't want to let Grace down.

Her heart was pounding like never before. She swallowed as the cameraman started counting down, "Three . . . two . . . one . . . rolling."

Grace wanted to capture every important event leading up to the party, and choosing the *chambelán* was number one on the list. "In the event that he says no," Grace had added as a side note, "we can always cut it out." *Great*, Fabi thought.

Now Fabi took a deep breath and entered the gymnasium. The room smelled of pine-scented disinfectant. Basketballs were bouncing across the floor. Students were shouting, as the class was in the middle of basketball drills. She couldn't believe that she was actually going to do this — in front of *everyone*. The camera was rolling. There was no way she could back out now.

The gym teacher noticed the camera and blew his whistle for attention. The students welcomed the break. They lined up on their numbers on the floor. Fabi saw Milo and tried to wave. He smiled back. His eyes lit up when he noticed the camera.

"Can I help you?" the gym teacher asked, smiling knowingly. Did everyone know?

Fabi tried to talk but her nerves were getting the better of her. Thankfully, Grace jumped in.

"Sorry to interrupt, sir. We're" — Grace motioned to the cameraman — "from *Quince Dreams*, a new reality TV show, and we're following Fabiola Garza around as she prepares for her quinceañera. There's a special boy here that she'd like to talk to."

The gym teacher motioned for her to proceed.

Slowly, Fabi walked down the line of students. All the boys smiled at her, hoping to be chosen to be the star of Fabi's show. Milo blushed as she came toward him. He was one of her best friends. She had him to thank for all of this. But that would have to wait until later. Right now she had to focus on her show. Fabi stopped in front of Daniel. He stared back at her with a surprised expression. Her nerves jammed her senses. This was a mistake, she thought. They'd just met. What if he laughed? What if he said no? What was she thinking? He was out of her league — way too cool for her. Fabi tried to step back, but Grace was right behind her.

"Um, Daniel, hi."

"Hi," he said back.

"Um, I was thinking. Wondering, actually. So I have this party and I need a *chambelán*. So how about it?"

The room was completely silent as everyone leaned in to hear his response. Daniel glanced quickly around the room and then at the camera that was focused on his face. He turned bright red. Fabi's heart was racing. She started to feel faint. Daniel looked at Fabi and smiled weakly.

"Sure," he said shyly. The crowd whooped and hollered in approval.

Fabi jumped excitedly with relief and gave him a hug. "Thank you. Thank you, thank you," she said. Students rushed up to them in congratulations. The rest of the kids made signs with their hands and waved at the camera. Over their heads, Fabi looked for Milo. But she couldn't find him anywhere.

chapter 7

The rest of the week whirled by. Grace stuck to Fabi like Velcro, attending all of her classes and interviewing classmates, teachers, and even the lunch lady. Fabi loved all the attention. Her heart was bursting at the seams. She didn't know life could be so good — she wished that every week could be this amazing! But by Friday, Fabi was looking forward to a break. *Who knew that being a TV celebrity was so draining?*

Grace dropped Fabi off at the restaurant after school. She had to meet with her director and promised to swing by later. As she was about to enter the family restaurant, Fabi heard the sounds of people arguing. It was coming from around back. The voices sounded familiar, so she decided to check it out.

Fabi poked her head around the building, into the dirt alley behind the restaurant. She ignored the graffiti covering the exterior. She'd already painted over the tags three times in the last couple of months. A freshly painted wall just tempted every boy in town to make public his love for his girlfriend by spraypainting a big heart with "Juanito loves Juanita" (or whatever) inside.

The angry voices grew louder — and one of them belonged to her cousin Santiago. She was about to charge into the backyard, but then she caught a glimpse of the Salinas brothers and she ducked back behind the wooden fence. Their backs were to her, so they didn't see her. Ever so slowly, she peeked around the gate.

"You can't hide from us, man," Brandon Salinas said. He had Santiago by the shirt collar and shook him roughly. His dopey-looking brother, Travis, was standing next to him.

"Yeah, man, you can't hide," added Travis.

Fabi grew nervous. The Salinas brothers were trouble. Ever since they were small, they were always stealing bikes or beating up younger kids for their candies or shoes. Now that they were bigger, she knew whatever they were up to couldn't be good.

"Guys," Santiago began. He smiled as he wiggled free from Brandon's grip. Her cousin looked tired. There was a heavy trash bag at his feet. Santiago glanced over his shoulder toward the back door of the restaurant and lowered his voice. "I already told you. I'm not into that stuff anymore. Leave me alone, all right?"

Brandon spat on the ground. "What? You think you can just drop out and no one would notice? We had a deal, man, and we want what's ours."

"Yeah, you can't drop out," Travis echoed.

Santiago looked over Brandon's shoulder. Brandon noticed and turned his head in Fabi's direction. *Darn*, she thought. Fabi took a step into the clearing, unsure of what to do next.

Santiago leaned in to the Salinas brothers. "Look, I can't talk now. Not here. I'll call you guys tonight. I promise."

Brandon looked at Fabi, then nodded to

Santiago. "All right, but you better call. I don't like chasing your punk ass."

"Yeah, punk," repeated his brother.

The Salinas brothers walked toward Fabi. Brandon nodded to her as he passed. Travis also nodded. *What a bunch of dorks*, Fabi thought. But they had big egos and guns, and that made them dangerous. Fabi feared that her cousin was in way over his head.

When they left, Fabi walked over to Santiago. He was throwing the trash bag into the Dumpster in the alley.

"Everything all right?" she asked, knowing that things definitely weren't.

Santiago looked down the alley in the direction the Salinas brothers went. "Don't worry about it. I can handle them."

"Santiago —" Her voice cracked, revealing her anxiety. "I know it's none of my business, but I'm really worried about you. You've been lucky so far, but this can't go on. I'm serious."

"Don't you think I know that?" Santiago snapped. Fabi jumped. "Don't you see me trying to change? I've been going to school and helping at the restaurant. I told those guys that I don't want to be involved in any more of their business. But you saw them," he said, gesturing down the alley. "They just won't let me be."

"But why don't you tell someone?" Fabi pleaded. "What about Officer Sanchez? Maybe he can help. Maybe he can get a restraining order or lock them up."

"That crap don't work. If I snitch on those guys, then they'll *really* come after me. Those fools know where I live." He kicked the dirt angrily. "It's not me that I'm worried about. I'd put my mom and all you in danger."

Santiago laughed, giving Fabi one of his signature "everything is cool" smiles. He turned over a milk crate and sat down, studying the ground. "You know what really sucks?"

"What?" Fabi grabbed another milk crate and sat next to him.

"When I was stuck in that mafioso's closet, I prayed. And you know me. I never pray. I prayed to La Virgen. I swore that if she got me out of that mess, I would change. And for a while it was going good. I've got this new cute English teacher from Chicago. I'm never late for her class." He chuckled softly. "My mom's even proud of me, you know?" He blew a curly lock from his face. "I used to think that if I made a lot of money, she could quit her job and be happy. But she was happier seeing me all dressed up like a stupid schoolboy, imagine that. She even got me some community college brochures. Ha! But it was all a dream, a lie. I guess I was just kidding myself. I'm a screwup, Fabi, and I'll always be one."

Fabi reached out to him, but was interrupted by a coughing sound. She looked up and saw Grace Cooper standing in the alley entrance. Grace smiled awkwardly.

"I'm sorry if I'm interrupting."

Santiago licked his lips, stood up, and brushed his pants. "Hey, you're the TV lady!" He'd switched on the charm as if nothing had just happened. Fabi didn't know how he could do that. "You're here to do a show on Fabiola. Ain't that right?"

Grace smiled brightly. "Why, yes, I am. Are you family?"

"Well, I don't like to brag," Santiago said, straightening up. "But I am her best-looking cousin."

Fabi smirked and swatted him on the stomach.

"What?" he said, pretending to be surprised. "It's true."

Grace smiled, enjoying the banter. "So will you be in the quince party?"

"For sure," Santiago said, breaking out into a little dance. "I've got moves."

Grace laughed at Santiago's antics. Then she looked at Fabi and the light dimmed in her eyes. She pulled out a manila envelope from her large leather handbag. "I'm really sorry to have to do this, but my boss really wants you to sign these documents."

"No problem," Fabi said, walking over to her.

"It's just some legal documents giving us permission to tape you at home and . . . " Her face fell completely, and Fabi became nervous. This couldn't be good. "There's no delicate way to say this. My boss wants permission to film you *if* you get sick."

Santiago shot Fabi a surprised look.

Fabi shrugged back at him. "Okay," she said.

"I'm really sorry. But he really wants to tape everything, you know."

This conversation was getting stranger and stranger. What was she talking about? But instead of asking, Fabi just nodded.

Grace let out a sigh of relief and smiled sadly. "Oh, Fabi, you're such a good sport. I really appreciate you letting us do this. You're a brave girl." She glanced at her watch. "Great! I've got to go. We want to get some shots of the town before the light goes. See you tomorrow." Grace waved and headed down the alley.

Santiago turned to her. "What was that all about?"

"Beats me," Fabi said, shaking her head in confusion. Something was up, and she couldn't shake the feeling that things were going seriously wrong. "But I know who does, and I'm getting to the bottom of it right now."

Fabi and Santiago entered the restaurant from the back. A Johnny Cash classic was playing on the old jukebox and customers were chattering excitedly. The usual clanging of pots came from the kitchen, where her father was busy preparing meals. Chuy was rushing between the *comal* and the counter, filling orders for more flour tortillas.

Chuy saw them and called out in Spanish, "Where you guys been? That TV lady was here looking for you."

"I saw her out back," Fabi said, gesturing to the alley.

Chuy nodded, then turned to Santiago. "Hey, those dishes aren't going to wash themselves."

Santiago grabbed Fabi's elbow and said, "Promise me you won't mention what you saw back there, you know, with the Salinas brothers. I meant it when I said I'd take care of it. I don't want you to worry about it, okay?"

"But, Santi —" Fabi protested.

He pinched her cheek softly. "You just focus on being amazing for the cameras. Okay, *guapa*?"

"Fine," she agreed. "Promise me you won't do anything crazy without talking to me first?"

Santiago smiled just as Mr. Garza repeated Chuy's request for him to wash the dishes. "Got to go. Boss man wants his dishes clean."

Fabi shook her head as Santiago hurried into the kitchen. She couldn't help but worry about her cousin. But this wasn't the time. Fabi looked across the room at her grandma Trini and Alexis. They were flipping through some fashion magazine and ripping out pictures they liked. She marched over to them to get some answers.

"Hey," Alexis said with a big smile, "what do you think of this dress? I like off the shoulders, but Grandma Trini wants a mermaid-style *dama* dress."

"I have to show off what God gave me," Grandma Trini said, gesturing to her bosom. "You know, before they go down to my knees." Alexis started to giggle. But Fabi wasn't laughing.

"What's the matter?"

"What's the matter?" Fabi cried. *"What's the matter?"* The customers nearest her stopped eating to see what was going on.

Grandma Trini smiled with a pained expression and pulled Fabi down into the chair next to her. The crowd lost interest and went back to socializing. "Who stuck a burr under your saddle?" Trini asked curtly. "This show is called *Quince Dreams*, not *Quince Malcriada*. We do all this for you and then we get yelled at like children."

Fabi was not going to let her grandmother bulldoze her into feeling guilty about something she didn't even do. Not now, when what she really needed were answers.

"Fine. I will not act like a brat. But you guys need to tell me what's really going on here. Why did Grace Cooper just give me a stack of release forms for when I get sick? And why does she keep saying that I'm a brave girl? What *exactly* did you guys say in that application?"

Grandma Trini and Alexis shared a glance. Then they both blushed as if caught in a lie. The hairs on Fabi's arms shot up. Was this all a lie?

"I want to see the letter you guys wrote," she said.

Alexis sighed. "Oh, what does it matter what we said? The important thing is that it's happening. In just two weeks you are going to have the biggest, coolest quinceañera in the Valley. People will be talking about it for years!"

Now Fabi knew she had reason to be *really* worried. "The letter!" she demanded, holding out her hand.

Alexis turned to Grandma Trini, who frowned as she reached into her bosom and pulled out a folded piece of paper. "It's only the rough draft," she said. "I kept it as a memento."

Fabi reached for it. But her grandmother wouldn't let it go. They tugged back and forth for a minute until Grandma Trini finally surrendered. "Fine. But we only did it because we love you. And we wanted you to have the quinceañera you deserve."

Fabi didn't want to hear the excuses. She wanted the facts. What exactly had her family gotten her into? Her hands started to shake as she unfolded the letter that was stained with Jean Naté perfume. Fabi bit her lower lip as she read. She noticed her sister's small handwriting.

Dear Quince Dreams,
    My name is Fabiola Garza. I am fifteen years old and my dream is to have a quinceañera.

Okay, she thought. *This doesn't sound too bad.* She continued to read.

For my whole life, I've taken care of others. I care for my little sister and brother like a mother, because my parents work real hard and don't have time. I care for my ailing grandmothers, who're very sick and can't take care of themselves. I take care of my cousin, who is a gang member and trying to get out of the thug life.

Okay, so that's stretching the truth a bit. But not horrible . . .

But I have a secret that my family doesn't know about. A secret that really scares me because I know that it will bring them much pain and difficulty. I am dying.

"Dying?!"
Alexis and Grandma Trini squirmed under Fabi's rage.
"We had to make it good!" Alexis cried.

I have a rare disease that the doctors don't know how to cure and they've only given me a month to live.

Fabi dropped the letter. She couldn't read any more. It disgusted her. How could they? How could they lie like that? But then the fog in her head cleared. The pieces fit into place. Grace's comment, the legal documents — it all made sense now. Grace thought that she was dying, and she wanted to give Fabi her last dying wish.

Her stomach knotted up and she balled her hands into tight fists. It was all a lie.

"Guys!" she cried, beside herself. "How could you do this? This is . . . this is . . . I don't know what this is, but it's wrong — so wrong. I can't believe you lied. Lied to *Quince Dreams*! When they find out . . ."

"How are they going to find out?" Alexis said. Her voice was light and indifferent. "We told them it was a secret. They won't mention anything to Mom and Dad, I know it."

"Mija." Grandma Trini grabbed Fabi's hand. "You saw the show. They want drama. That's how TV works. We just gave them what they wanted. They get their show. We get our quinceañera. Everyone is happy."

"But what happens when I don't die?" Fabi demanded. "Huh? Tell me that! What happens when they find out that it was all a lie?" She looked at her sister's and grandmother's blank faces. Fabi couldn't do this. She stood up. The letter stared up at her from the table. She felt sick just looking at it. Fabi crumbled the letter in her hands and stormed out of the restaurant.

Fabi waited until she'd walked down two blocks to let out a scream. She didn't care what people in the street thought. Right now, she was so upset at her sister and Grandma Trini that she wanted to rip out someone's hair. Her whole family had a knack for stirring up trouble. Fabi had to get away.

She turned onto one of the residential roads. Small houses with colorful wildflowers lined the block; bright sunflowers and tall bluebonnets adorned the metal gates. She breathed in the perfume of all the flowers, and a tear jerked from her eye. This had to be the worst nightmare of her entire life. Fabi watched a squirrel run up the trunk of a Mexican olive tree. She wished she could scurry up after it and hide forever in the trees. Her feet kept moving. How could she go back? How could she face Grace Cooper and everyone at school? What would she tell *Daniel*?

Fabi stormed into the park at the end of the street. Kids were playing in the playground. A group of men had gathered in the field to play baseball. Fabi found a bench that overlooked the field and sat down. She couldn't believe how low her grandmother and sister could go! Tears flowed freely down her cheeks. She thought about all the kids on TV commercials with shaved heads who were really dying. It wasn't something to joke about. Fabi covered her face with her hands. What was she going to do?

Just then a baseball came toward her. She picked it up. One of the guys who'd been playing came over to retrieve it.

"Fabi," he said, surprised.

She wiped her nose and looked up at Daniel.

"Are you all right?" he asked.

The concern on his face made her crumble. She couldn't hold back as tears sprang from her eyes. Daniel gently took the ball from her and passed it off to his friends, who continued the game without him. Then Daniel put his arms around her. Fabi was too frazzled by all the events to object and surrendered into the embrace.

When he released her, they sat down on the bench. Fabi didn't know what to say. She felt like an idiot, breaking down in front of Daniel like that.

"Hey," Daniel finally said, nudging her shoulder. "My mom always says that talking about your problems makes you feel better."

Fabi nodded, looking down at the crumpled paper still in her hand. She was just going to tell Daniel about the letter. But she found herself telling him everything. She started at the beginning, with her original plan to go to NYC with Georgia Rae. But when Alexis broke curfew a few weeks before, their dad had held Fabi responsible and forbade her to go anywhere. Then there was Melodee and the bet. Finally, she revealed the truth about *Quince Dreams* and how her sister and grandmother lied to get her on the show. When Fabi finished, she actually felt a lot better. He was right. It did feel better to tell someone.

Daniel stared out at the field, soaking in all

the information. He didn't say a word. His silence made Fabi nervous. Did he think she was a creep? "Wow," he finally said. "So you lied to get on that show, huh?"

Fabi nodded. "Do you think I'm an evil person?"

"You? No way. I don't think any of this is your fault. It's just . . . sometimes people do things that they think are right at the time because . . . because it's what they think they want."

"I know, I know," Fabi sighed, the weight of the situation barreling down on her. "I know Alexis and Grandma Trini didn't mean to hurt me. In their own way, they thought they were helping me. My mom and dad could never afford a fancy quinceañera. The restaurant is just barely making it, and if they didn't work so hard every day, we could lose everything. This whole situation is just . . . hard."

"Maybe if you explained it to the TV people, they'd understand."

"I doubt it." Fabi shook her head. "You should have seen Grace's face when she gave me the legal documents to sign. They think I'm dying from some terminal illness. They want a tear-jerking soap opera. They're not interested in my story. I'm just some girl from a small town, a loser."

Daniel reached out for Fabi's hand and squeezed it. The tender gesture took Fabi's breath away. His touch was warm and full of support. She'd never met anyone like him before.

"You're not a loser," he said with conviction. "And I don't ever want to hear you call yourself that. *I'm* the loser."

Fabi was shocked. She released his hand. What was he talking about? Daniel was the coolest guy she'd ever met — and the cutest, too. "What are you talking about?"

Daniel took a deep breath and continued to stare at the field. He was about to tell her something, but then changed his mind. "It's nothing. Forget about it."

Fabi stared at him. What was he about to say? Her mind started to race. Daniel turned to her and smiled.

"It's nothing," he repeated, trying to assure her. "I think you need to explain things to the show. Hey, maybe they'll do the show anyway. They're already here and they've spent all that money for the hall and the invitations. That woman still has to do a show, right?"

"Well, I guess that's all I can do," Fabi said, trying to sound more confident than she felt. She took a deep breath. The air was sweet. Fabi smiled at Daniel. No more lies. It was time to tell the truth and accept the consequences.

chapter 8

Fabi tried to talk to Grace several times throughout that next week. But Grace was in McAllen a lot, setting up logistics and the celebrity assistants. The fashion designer was very demanding of Fabi's time. She was a humorless perfectionist, changing Fabi's dress designs more times than the wind changed directions.

When the dance instructor called for the first practice session, Fabi welcomed the break. She missed her old life, missed serving her grandpa Frank and listening to his stories about the war, missed the smell of her dad's cooking and all the gossip that spun from her *abuelita* Alpha's lips. But the party was only a week away, and Fabi half hoped that maybe the longer she waited, the more likely Grace would let her have the party — despite the lie.

They were supposed to meet the dance instructor in the Dos Rios High gymnasium after school. The principal was more than happy to let them use the space for free. Alexis, Grandma Trini, and Fabi arrived early. When Georgia Rae walked through the door, it was like a breath of fresh air. It felt like years since they'd hung out. Fabi had tried to tell Georgia Rae about the lie and her mixed feelings about going along with rehearsals on the phone, but Georgia Rae was too excited to share Fabi's concern. A chance to be on national TV was an opportunity that only came once in a lifetime, she cheered.

"I'm here," Georgia Rae exclaimed, walking into the gymnasium with a brand-new hairstyle. She'd blow-dried her hair super straight and added red highlights. "You like?" she asked, striking a pose in her new 'do.

"Ay, mija," Grandma Trini admired. "You look so fancy, just like a real pop singer on the TV."

Fabi had to agree Georgia Rae looked good. Fabi wondered if maybe it was time for her to get a new look, too.

They all turned when they heard boisterous laughter coming from the hallway. Fabi held her breath as Santiago and Daniel walked in with an older man with salt-and-pepper hair and a short goatee. The man, holding a fancy boom box, had to be the choreographer, she thought. But who were the three girls trailing behind them? Then she recognized Violet, Noelia, and Mona. *What are they doing here?* Her body stiffened. Fabi hadn't invited them to be in her quince; she technically didn't invite anyone, but now she felt her ears burn. Would they be upset?

Noelia smiled and called, "Hey, Fabi, we found them wandering the halls."

"Yeah," added Violet. "We were just telling Mr. Cardoza about the dance we made up for the talent show last fall."

"Did you know that he taught J. Lo how to dance?" Mona said in disbelief.

"I hope you don't mind —" Noelia looked a tad embarrassed.

"But we want to watch," finished Violet.

Mr. Cardoza — clearly that was the goateed choreographer guy — looked at the girls as if they'd just said the craziest thing in the world. "Watch?" He shook his head dramatically. "Three fine dancers like yourselves can't watch. Not in my practice. You ladies will practice with us. You" — he pointed to Noelia — "will be Fabi's understudy."

Fabi was confused. They only had three guys.

Mr. Cardoza looked at Fabi and said, "I read your story. If you're not up to dancing, one of these girls can fill in for you. Now, kids, gather around me." He motioned for everyone to come over. The three girls screamed excitedly as they joined the group. Mr. Cardoza noticed Grandma Trini and nodded. "Ma'am," he said to her, "with all due respect, my dancing style is very rigorous. I am a demanding instructor. I don't accept excuses or Bengay breaks. My technique is not for the innocent. It has been called *raunchy* by some and *vulgar* by others. How do you think J. Lo got that butt?" No one answered. "My question for you is, do you think you can keep up?"

Grandma Trini kicked one leg up in the air and dropped down into a split. *"Mijo,"* she said from the floor. "If I can dance with the devil and live to tell about it, I can do your dirty dance."

The choreographer burst into a cheerful laugh. "Yes! That was exactly what I wanted to hear. Okay, now let's start with a warm-up. You guys like to Zumba?"

"Wait!" Fabi interrupted. "We're not all here. We're missing one person." She looked at Georgia Rae and Alexis. "Milo's not here!"

Georgia Rae shrugged.

Mr. Cardoza clapped his hands for attention. "I will let you interrupt once, because you are the quinceañera. But that's it. My time is valuable. I won't wait for no one. Not even for you, my sweet. Like I said, one of these girls will fill in for whoever can't keep up."

"But they're girls," Fabi said flatly.

Mr. Cardoza raised up two fingers in a threatening manner. "Now, where was I?" He turned on his boom box. Reggaeton dance beats blasted out of the speakers. "All right, everybody. I want you to stick your booty out like *this* and shake them hips!"

• • •

The next day, Fabi's thighs screamed in pain when she tried to get out of bed. Thankfully, it was Saturday and she didn't have to go to work until the afternoon. Her whole body ached from the rigorous dance workout. Every muscle cried out for relief. She smiled to herself, staring up at the ceiling, remembering how Grandma Trini put everyone to shame with her serpentine stomach rolls. Her smile faded when she thought about Milo. He hadn't shown up at all. She racked her brain, trying to think if she'd somehow insulted him by mistake. Nothing came to mind. Was he mad about Daniel being her *chambelán*? Sure, he'd offered at the beginning. But he was just being nice, just trying to help her out. He couldn't possibly be upset about that!

Fabi took two quick breaths, willed herself past the pain, and got up. This would not be easy, she thought, grabbing muscle-relieving cream from her nightstand — *ouch!*

She borrowed Santiago's truck and drove to the trailer park where Milo lived. Milo's house was the last one down the first row. There were fake flowers planted in front. He said his mom preferred the synthetic ones because they were the only flowers that didn't die on her. Fabi walked around back and knocked on his bedroom window. Milo poked his head out from behind a dark curtain. He had his headphones on. She motioned for him to come out.

Fabi licked her lips nervously. On the ride over she'd tried to think of what to say. But the truck kept stalling on her when she tried to shift too quickly, so she hadn't come up with anything good.

Milo opened the front door. Fabi couldn't help but peek inside. She'd never been invited into his house. He always made excuses about it being messy. This time, Fabi saw a woman passed out on the couch. She was missing a green sandal and there was a bottle of Jack Daniel's on the floor. Quickly, Fabi looked away, hoping Milo hadn't noticed her prying.

"Hey," he said softly, closing the door behind him.

"Hey," Fabi said back.

"What's up?"

She shrugged. "Not much. We missed you yesterday at the quinceañera practice. You didn't call or anything."

Milo said nothing. He glanced back at the house, then stared off over Fabi's shoulder.

Fabi wondered about Milo's family. He never talked about them. "Do you want to walk?" she asked.

Milo nodded. They hopped through the hole in the chain-link fence that led to an open field. It was private property, but no one ever came around there. For a while, the only sounds were the crunching of their feet on the dried grass. The deeper they went, the more the desert landscape opened up to them. A slight breeze tossed Fabi's hair, providing a welcome break from the stifling heat. She watched a bird soar high up above. It was so peaceful here, she thought.

"I don't think I can be in the quinceañera," Milo said softly, breaking the silence.

"What? Are you crazy?" Fabi stared at him in shock. She had not expected this. "But . . . this party is partly your fault. You can't back out. I know you helped Grandma Trini and Alexis write that letter."

Milo sucked in his teeth. "You found out that you're dying. I knew it was a bad idea. I told them not to put that in," he said, looking sincere. "But I was outvoted, two to one. Your sister can be pretty pushy once she gets her heart set on something."

"You could have told me."

"I wanted to, but then you got chosen and . . . I didn't get a chance."

Fabi understood. She'd been trying to talk to Grace, but something always came up. Time was slipping away. Fabi had to tell her before it got too late. Fabi thought about Milo's mom passed out on the couch. "Is everything okay? I mean, at home with your mom?"

Milo looked sideways at her as they walked. "You saw that?"

She nodded.

"She'll be all right. I think she got fired last night from her job at the HEB grocery store. Don't worry. She'll be fine by tomorrow," he said in a matter-of-fact tone.

His nonchalant attitude made Fabi feel more like a stranger than a friend. She couldn't understand the distance that was swelling up between them. They'd gone from sharing their deepest feelings to awkward silence in a matter of days. She also realized that there was more to Milo than she thought. She cared about him and didn't want to lose his friendship.

"Did I do something to make you mad?" she asked.

"It's nothing," he said, but Milo's voice was tight.

"It's just that we were super close."

"Fabi."

"You used to come to the restaurant after school and now you won't even talk to me. If I did something, tell me."

Milo shook his head. He grabbed a rusty beer can and threw it. It didn't go very far.

"Milo," Fabi tried again, softer.

"I don't want to talk about it, okay? I just need some time to myself, that's all."

"Time to yourself?" She was starting to grow annoyed by his attitude. "I thought we were friends. Friends talk to each other, right?" She found herself getting really mad. "Is this about Daniel?" When Milo said nothing, Fabi continued. "Daniel's cool. You'd like him. I swear, if you'd just come to the rehearsal, you'd see."

"You don't even know that boy," Milo said, looking at her out of the corner of his eye.

"Where does he come from? Who are his friends? You know nothing about him. He just appeared, and now you're making him your *chambelán*." Milo took a long breath. "I was there for you when no else was. I was your friend when Dex tried to push you around, remember that? You've changed. Now that you're going to be on TV, you're like Ms. Popularity. How do you know that he's not just using you? I saw him at the mall talking to Melodee."

Fabi jerked back. Why was he saying these things? "That's his job!" she stammered. "He works at the pizzeria. He has to be nice to everyone."

Milo shook his head. "I don't like him, and there's nothing you can say that'll change that."

"You're just jealous," Fabi said, feeling frustrated and annoyed. Why was Milo acting like this?

"Jealous?" Milo started to laugh.

Fabi looked straight at him, trying to read his expression. How could he laugh? How could he be so mean? The mocking look on his face made her blood boil. "You know what?" she said angrily. "Forget it. You're right. I don't need you. I don't even know why I bother." She turned away. "If you're going to act like this, then I'd rather you didn't come to my quinceañera at all."

Fabi walked back to the truck. A part of her hoped that Milo would call her back, apologize, grab her, anything. He didn't. She slowed her pace. He wasn't going to call her back. Fabi didn't want to leave things like this, but what else could she do?

For the next few days, Fabi forced herself not to think about Milo. There were many more pressing things at the moment. She thought about Daniel's advice.

Maybe Grace will understand. She may even let me have the quinceañera, she hoped, pushing open the front door of her family's restaurant. Just when Fabi didn't think things could get any worse, they did. As she walked in, she stepped into the middle of an ugly argument between none other than her father and Grace Cooper.

"You get that *sinvergüenza* out of my restaurant right now!" he cried, waving a skillet in the air threateningly. Chuy and Santiago were holding Leonardo at bay in the kitchen. Fabi had never seen her father so upset before. She turned to her mother, who held her arm across Grace like a protective shield. Grandma Trini and Alexis were trying to reassure Grace that everything was all right and not to worry.

"I'm so sorry, Mr. Garza," Grace said pleadingly. "My assistant was supposed to tell you. I didn't mean —"

"Didn't mean . . . I'm sorry . . . Is that why you went behind my back and paid that fool BJ to cater my daughter's quinceañera?"

Fabi jumped back. Not BJ Lujan — of the restaurant Los Granos de Mama! They used recycled old lard in their food; everyone knew that!

Grace lowered her head in defeat. BJ Lujan had been trying for years to steal Garza's recipe for chili con carne. Everyone knew that it was the best. He'd even gone to great lengths to trick them, by planting a serving girl to spy for him.

Fabi looked at Grace, praying that what her dad said wasn't true.

"*Pues*, then I am not going," her father stated, sweating profusely.

"Please, Leonardo," her mother protested. "You don't know what you're saying. This is

Fabi's quinceañera. It's going to be on TV. Every —"

"I don't care," her father said, pressing his hand to his chest. "I have my *orgullo* and no one will take that from me. I will not be disrespected at my daughter's quinceañera. *¡Saca a esa vieja!* I don't want to look at her."

Grace pulled out her cell phone. "I'm so sorry. Let me call my assistant and maybe we can —"

"I told you to get her out of here!" Her father struggled with Chuy and Santiago. Mr. Garza was a big man, and it looked like he would get free when all of a sudden he cried out in pain. His eyes grew big while his face went pale. Leonardo clutched his right arm and collapsed to the floor, bringing Santiago and Chuy down with him.

"Mom!" Fabi cried, running over to her father. "Mom! Dad isn't moving!" She turned around and saw her mother standing frozen in place, stiff like Grandpa Frank's starched pants. No one moved. "Alexis! Call 911. Call 911 right now."

"Help!" Santiago cried. "Tío weighs a ton. He's squishing my leg."

Chuy and Fabi helped Santiago free himself from under Leonardo.

"Is he dead?" Abuelita Alpha asked, pulling out her rosary.

Fabi's mother had regained her composure and snapped, "Don't you dare say that! He's not dead." She rushed over to Leonardo's side and began to cry. Alexis put her arm around her mother and said comforting words.

"*Pues*, he's not moving. *Se puede morir del coraje*," Fabi's grandmother Alpha explained.

Grace sprang to Fabi's side. "The ambulance is on the way. I'm so sorry. I feel responsible. This is not what I intended. Fabi, you have to believe me. I just thought they could relax and enjoy the day. I'm sorry." Tears started to well up in her eyes. "I didn't think. I didn't —"

Fabi wanted to comfort her. She wanted to tell her that it was all right, that her father would be okay. But her dad was on the floor. He'd had some kind of attack. It was not all right!

The ambulance showed up and rushed Leonardo Garza to a hospital in McAllen. The family piled into cars to follow the blinking lights of the emergency mobile. *This was not supposed to happen*, Fabi thought, sitting in the back of her grandma Trini's car.

No one uttered a word on the drive. Grandma Trini didn't even turn on the radio. Fabi watched the darkening sky. She was numb. Her sister was sniveling next to her. There was the clicking of rosary beads rubbing together as Abuelita Alpha mumbled prayers in the front seat. For once, Grandma Trini didn't complain and prayed alongside her silently.

A chill set into Fabi's bones. She couldn't shake the feeling that this was all her fault.

chapter 9

Leonardo was okay. He'd experienced a minor heart attack, but was recovering nicely. The doctors wanted to keep him for a few days to make sure his vital signs went back to normal. Fabi's father had ignored his doctor's past advice, and now it was catching up with him. The doctor prescribed a change in diet, daily exercise, and no stress. By the end of the week, Leonardo was finally home. Fabi promised herself that she would do everything in her power to make her dad's recovery as peaceful as possible.

Chuy took over head-cook responsibilities. Fabi assisted between school, practice, and her other quince duties. She knew that she had to explain the truth to Grace. But there were always new things that had to be ordered, cleaned, or thrown out at the restaurant, which just couldn't wait. It wasn't until Grace approached her about Melodee's quinceañera that she realized that now it might be too late.

"Do you think she would mind if we tagged along with you today?" Grace asked, sitting across the table from Fabi on Fabi's fifteen-minute break.

Today was Melodee's quinceañera! With everything going on, Fabi had totally forgotten about it. *Great*, she thought, as she smiled at Grace from across the table. "Sure, I don't think she'll mind."

"Wonderful," Grace said as she scribbled some notes down on a pad. "We just want to get some shots of other quinceañeras for a promo piece." She reached out for Fabi's hand. "How is your dad feeling?"

"He's much better. He started getting around with this walker Abuelita Alpha lent him. He complains a lot. That's always a good sign."

Grace smiled. "I feel so bad about the whole thing, you know? It wasn't our intention —"

"I know," Fabi said, looking down at the plastic red tabletop. There was a dried salsa stain on the edge of the table. Fabi pulled a wet rag from her apron pocket and started to rub at the stain. It was time to come clean, she resolved. She had to tell Grace, now, before anything worse happened. "There's something I need to tell you," Fabi began.

"I know what you're going to say," Grace cut in.

Grace gave Fabi a small smile. "None of this is your fault. I don't want you to blame yourself. You should see the video footage we have of your dad." Grace wiped away a tear with the back of her hand. "He's really very proud of you. This day means a lot to him. He never believed that he could provide for you and your sister the way you deserved. This party means so much to him."

Fabi felt her heart stretch in a hundred directions. It was exhausting just to think of everyone who was now affected by this party. This was no longer about winning some stupid bet. Fabi's quinceañera had become the culmination, the dream, of every person she had ever known — a dream built with the past generations' blood, sweat, and hope. It was a dream for a better tomorrow. A quinceañera's dream. But this dream was quickly becoming Fabi's cross to bear.

"So I'll pick you up around four?" Grace asked.

"Yeah, sure," Fabi said, without enthusiasm.

Grace left and Fabi reached for her phone and dialed Georgia Rae's number. How could she forget Melodee's quinceañera? What was she going to wear? She glanced at her watch. It was already two o'clock. No, this was not happening!

Thankfully, her friend picked up on the second ring. "Georgia Rae," Fabi cried, touching her head. When was the last time she'd washed her hair? she wondered. And now she didn't have enough time! Her heart began to race. "What are you doing? Whatever it is — stop! We have an emergency. It's Melodee's quinceañera. Yes! Today. I know. I'm freaking out. I need you here, now."

When Fabi hung up, she noticed Grandma Trini and Alexis standing next to her. When had they appeared?

"We heard," Alexis said in a serious tone.

"We are here for you, *mija*," Grandma Trini assured, placing her hand on Fabi's arm. "*Esa* fashion lady left a bunch of dresses at my house that she'd made and no like. Let's go and try them on. I can hem anything not finished. That way we all look pretty for the party."

"We?"

Alexis rolled her eyes. "Well, yeah, of course we're going to go with you. We won't let you go alone. Let me call Santiago and Chuy."

"No, wait!" Fabi grabbed her by the arm. "I only got one invitation. And now I'm bringing five guests." She raised her hand for emphasis. "Three's plenty. Besides, someone has to run the restaurant while we're out."

"Don't you worry about the restaurant," Grandpa Frank called out from the counter. Her grandfather turned his veterans' cap backward and shot her a wink. "C'mon, boys," he said, gesturing to his buddies sitting along the counter. "It'll be just like old times in the barracks."

Fabi smiled with pride at her grandfather and the senior brigade. The old men started to tease one another as they familiarized themselves with the kitchen. It felt good to have their support.

"And I'll make some of my famous chili," Abuelita Alpha exclaimed, heading into the kitchen. It seemed like everyone wanted to help. Fabi wished she could stay and hang out with them. But the clock was ticking and she had to start getting ready for the first part of the quinceañera showdown.

Grandma Trini, Alexis, Georgia Rae, and Fabi arrived at Melodee's quinceañera after four. They looked more like a gang than guests. All four of them chose the same reject *dama* dress. Alexis thought it was a good idea. It would show their unity, but Fabi knew that it was really because it was the best one in the lot. The designer called the color "burnt fuchsia." She swore it was up-and-coming. The dress hung off one shoulder and had a cute bubble hem skirt that ended above the knee. Fabi wasn't crazy about the big rose on the shoulder, but there was no time to remove it. Fabi met Grace and the cameraman at the door of the McAllen Convention Center.

The convention center was a colossal exposition space where the hottest singers and shows performed. Fabi had come once with Georgia Rae to see *The Lion King*. She couldn't help but feel a little excited to be there again. The majestic building made everything feel so much more special.

Melodee's party was already in full swing. There was valet parking with a real red carpet, and a mariachi group was playing as the guests arrived. Fabi smiled shyly at Grace.

Grace noticed and squeezed Fabi's hand. "Don't worry. Yours will be better."

They followed the crowd into the convention center and toward the ballroom. Georgia Rae came up behind Fabi and pinched her.

"Hey, notice anything?"

Fabi glanced around at the other guests. Everyone was dressed in suits and cute dresses. "No, what?" Fabi whispered back.

"Everyone is wearing black and white."

Fabi looked again and noticed that Georgia Rae was right. Georgia Rae asked to see the invitation.

"Damn it," Georgia Rae cursed under her

breath. "Look, it says here it's a Black-and-White Affair. That's the theme."

"No way," Fabi said under her breath. She had hoped to go unnoticed at the party.

"Too late now." Alexis shrugged. "I don't care. So we stand out."

As they got closer to the ballroom, Fabi's hands started to tremble. She couldn't calm them or her heartbeat down. "Let's just check it out and leave. I don't want to stick around."

Grandma Trini, who had been unusually quiet up until now, cleared her throat loudly. *"Al mal tiempo buena cara."*

Georgia Rae looked at her blankly.

Grandma Trini smiled brightly. "We must show a good face even if we really dislike the situation." The girls nodded, with smiles as big as Texas. "Fabi, you will bring over this gift," Trini said, removing a beautifully wrapped box from her purse.

"Gift? Grandma, we didn't get her a gift."

"I know," Trini said, "I just wrapped this ceramic pink elephant your grandma Alpha gave me last Christmas." She made a face.

Fabi laughed, taking the package. At that moment, she had a burst of love for the crazy old lady with too much perfume.

Grandma Trini motioned with her fingers when she talked. "Then we go over and congratulate the quinceañera and her family, eat some food, and leave. In that order." The girls nodded. "And if we're going to stand out," she added, turning toward the entrance of the ballroom, "we hold our heads up high and walk with style."

Georgia Rae, Alexis, and Fabi laughed as they watched Grandma Trini step into the hall like she owned the place. They nodded to one another and strutted into Melodee Stanton's quinceañera like they were Dos Rios royalty.

Electronica pop dance music shook the walls of the ballroom. Fabi stood by the chocolate fondue fountain, her mouth open in awe. The huge open space looked elegant, with rich red carpeting on the floor and an amazing lighting system that shot designs of colors on three of the walls. On the fourth wall, overlooking the eight-foot quince party's table, was a photo-montage of Melodee.

"Ooh, look," Fabi's grandmother cried, and pointed to the ceiling. Dangling up above was a dazzling chandelier made out of crystals in the shape of a butterfly with its wings spread out.

There had to be at least two hundred people there, Fabi thought, looking around the room. The tables were decorated with tall, curly willow-branch centerpieces that sparkled with little white flowers and candles. Each place setting had a personalized name card. There were two cake tables and a mountain of gifts piled up in between. Guests were talking adamantly with one another, hanging out at the bar, or mingling on the dance floor.

Fabi really, really wanted to leave.

There was a harsh scratching sound from the speaker and everyone stopped talking. Melodee came through a side door. Her quince party streamed in behind her. Everyone started to clap. She was wearing a strapless chiffon and satin black-and-white evening gown with a lacy beaded top. An elegant tiara was placed on top of her loose blonde curls.

There was a glass of champagne in Melodee's hand. Fabi wondered if she was drunk.

Melodee grabbed the mic. "Is this stupid thing on?" she said to the sound guy. He gave her the thumbs-up. Melodee smiled as she stared across the dance floor. Her gaze stopped at Fabi. "Well, it's time for the fun to begin. I see that all the guests have arrived."

Fabi groaned to herself. She had a terrible feeling about this. There she was, standing out like a red stoplight. Georgia Rae and Alexis reached for her hands at the same time for support. Fabi was grateful to have them there.

"First things first," Melodee continued in her annoying, singsong voice. "I'd love to thank my dear mother and father for paying for this fabulous party." The guests clapped politely. "I want to thank Fabiola Garza for having the courage to come to my party and bring the TV camera. I promise you a good show," she said to the cameraman. "I also wanted to give Fabi a small token of my appreciation, because honestly I don't think I would have had as much fun organizing this day without a good reason."

One of Melodee's *damas* brought a wrapped gift over to Fabi. The guests cheered again for Melodee as she blew Fabi an air-kiss. The crowd approved and clapped even louder.

Fabi pulled off the black ribbon and opened the box. Inside, there was a brand-new electric razor — the kind you'd use to shave your head. This was horrible. Melodee smiled devilishly from across the room. A guy behind Fabi started to laugh.

"Oh, and let me not forget one last person." There was movement behind Melodee. Someone was moving forward. "I would like to thank my handsome, sweet, hopelessly devoted new boyfriend for being here today. You made my victory possible. Thank you, my love. Daniel Cruz."

Fabi's breath caught in her throat. Did she hear right? But yes — she watched in horror as Daniel appeared at Melodee's side. Daniel!

Fabi's whole world shattered. It felt like a dozen fishing hooks pierced and pulled sharply at her chest, tearing apart her heart.

"Hey," Georgia Rae asked, "isn't that *your chambelán*?"

It took Fabi a couple of seconds to react. Fat tears started to stream down her cheeks. This was the worst humiliation in the world. The crowd turned to look at Fabi's reaction as if this was a big joke that everyone was in on but her.

Onstage, Daniel stared down at his shoes. Melodee didn't seem to notice or care. She turned to him and gave him a long kiss on the lips.

"Ah yes, my boyfriend," Melodee slurred, as she put one arm around him, "who is so hopelessly devoted to me that he would do anything to make me happy. Isn't that right?" she asked him. Daniel smiled back in confirmation.

"You!" Fabi cried. A flood of angry words came to her mind. A woman grunted loudly in disapproval next to her, jerking Fabi back from her fury. Then she noticed the looks of disbelief and frowns aimed right at her — as if she'd done something wrong!

Melodee smiled as she swung her head back to Fabi. "Is that camera rolling?"

Grace nodded that it was. She had to get Grace out of there, Fabi thought, but everything was happening too quickly.

Melodee continued without missing a beat. "Please excuse Miss Fabiola Garza. It's not her fault she has no manners. How 'bout we have some music while the waiters bring out the food?" The guests returned to their celebratory mood, ignoring Fabi's outburst.

Fabi turned to Georgia Rae. But she didn't know what to say. She was numb with disbelief. Then Melodee started walking toward Fabi. She was dragging Daniel by the hand behind her. Fabi's breath caught. *What is she going to do now?*

Melodee smirked as she passed Fabi, Grandma Trini, Alexis, and Georgia Rae in their matching outfits. She finally stopped in front of Grace and the camera. Fabi's heart was beating wildly. Daniel was standing right behind Melodee, totally ignoring Fabi three feet away. Melodee smiled at the camera and said, "I think it's ironic that your show is called *Quince Dreams*. It's ironic because that's all it really is, for Fatty. A dream. Your quince plans . . . all a dream." Melodee sighed deeply, and glanced at Fabi. "I told you not to mess with me."

Grace turned to look at Fabi. "What is she talking about?"

"Ha!" cried Melodee. "That's a good question . . . what am I talking about?" She reached back and grabbed Daniel's hand. "See, my boyfriend here told me all about how you LIED to the TV producers to get on their show."

Grace stared at Fabi. Her eyes were begging her to tell her it wasn't true. Fabi didn't know what to say. What could she say?

"Oh, yeah, Fabi's not dying," Melodee sneered to Grace. "No, that would be too good. No, dear old Fabi is just pathetic, a liar, and a loser. So pathetic that she had to lie about dying to get any attention. So pathetic that she believed that my boyfriend —"

Not another word, Fabi thought, pressing her hands to her ears. She ran out of the ballroom with Melodee's words still ringing in her head. Tears still flowed down her face. But she didn't bother to wipe them away. This was the cruelest thing she'd ever experienced. It was the most horrible day of her life. Fabi started to run through the parking lot, but her heels made it difficult so she took them off. She thought about carrying them, but she was so mad that she flung them at the convention center as she cursed.

Fabi hurried down the block not wanting to see anyone. Maybe she could go to Mexico. Disappear across the border. Fabi didn't know where to go; she headed north instead, away from her family and friends, away from her life.

chapter 10

The miserable heat baked Fabi's back and made the sidewalk feel like she was walking on hot coals. But she felt numb to it all. Cars kicked dirt in her face as they passed her on the street. Her dress was too tight and itched as it stuck to her skin. Fabi was out of breath and her skin burned. Downtown McAllen was undergoing mass revitalization with big boxy chain stores lining up and down the block. The franchise area soon disappeared behind her, giving way to an open orange grove.

It was one of the last groves left in the growing city. Farm owners found it more profitable to sell off their land to speculators than grow a crop. It was about ten degrees cooler under the trees, which provided welcome shade.

Fabi stopped and picked an orange. It was bittersweet. The juices ran down her mouth, reminding her of when she was small and her dad would bring back fruit from the local harvest. Life was so simple then. She craved those times. A car honk made her look up. Grandma Trini lowered the window in her SUV that she'd parked alongside the road.

"Ay, mija," she said softly. "Are you okay?"

Fabi stared blankly as her grandmother hopped out of the raised Chevy Tahoe, leaving Alexis and Georgia Rae in the backseat. It didn't seem real. It was too painful to be real: Melodee's party, Daniel her boyfriend, Grace's face when she learned the truth. Fabi wanted to wake from this horrible quince dream.

But seeing her grandmother walk toward her in her big matted hairdo, fuchsia dress, and matching chunky earrings was proof enough that it wasn't a dream. For some crazy reason, despite all the horribly embarrassing things that had happened today, Fabi realized that her family would always be there for her. Fabi couldn't stop herself from laughing. Thoughts of Milo and Alexis defending her against Melodee, talking to Daniel in the library, Melodee in the restroom, the TV camera, and everything else played out like a movie. *What was it all for?* she thought. She didn't realize how much stress she'd been holding back until now. It felt good to laugh, like shedding off old skin.

"We've made a mess of things, haven't we?" she said to her grandma.

"*Nos cacharon*. They caught us." Her grandmother paused to grab an orange and then started to peel it with her long painted nails. She took a deep breath and looked down the row of low-hanging trees. "I met your grandfather here in a grove like this. A woman who read cards told me that I would meet an ugly man who smelled of citrus with a honey tongue." Grandma Trini blushed. "She said that I would give him many babies. At first I thought she was cursing me, because I dated her son. But when Rafa sang to me on top of a ladder, I knew that psychic was the real deal."

Fabi smiled. Lil Rafa, her deceased grandfather, had not been a handsome man, but he'd had a beautiful voice. Still, she didn't quite understand why her grandmother was telling her this story. Trini walked over and pulled her into a hug.

"I'm sorry, *chiquita*," she said, pressing Fabi's head to her big bosom. "I don't know why I remembered that story. It was just . . . seeing you there . . . hearing you being torn apart *como una cualquiera* reminded me of when I was young and how the mean girls used to say *cosas feas* to me."

"Really, Grandma?"

"Oh, yeah." She laughed. "We were really poor back then. We didn't have electricity or even a floor. *Pura tierra.*" She stomped the earth to demonstrate her point. "I didn't even have shoes to go to school. But I always had pretty dresses. I knew how to sew," she said proudly. "And I was good. I would go to the factories at night and grab the scraps from the Dumpsters and make the most beautiful dresses. I put *esas ricas* to shame." She smiled brightly. "And of course they were jealous because I was a double D in junior high and those girls only had mosquito bites on their chests."

Fabi laughed.

"But they knew how to hurt me without leaving bruises on the outside. They used their words. I still carry those wounds." Grandma Trini raised her hand to her chest.

"What did you do?" Fabi asked.

"I went to a *bruja*, a card reader. I wanted to use words and hurt them, too. I didn't go to school, so I didn't know how to fight them on their level. But I was so angry. I wanted to hex them, make their hair fall out."

Fabi smiled, enjoying her grandmother's story. "And what happened?"

Grandma Trini finished off the last orange slice. "The card reader told me about your grandfather, and my life changed for the better. And when Lil Rafa became a famous singer, that became my revenge. Those women are all old and falling apart now. I see them sometimes. Their hearts became all wrinkly like a dried prune with all that hate and venom. Now when I see them I hold my head up high. I shake my big head of hair, which you know is all mine, and I show them that my life turned out grand."

Fabi smiled, happy for her grandmother. "Maybe I need to see that *bruja*," she said, only half joking.

"That's a great idea," her grandmother agreed, slapping her arm. It was kind of hard, but her grandmother didn't notice; her eyes were glazed over in thought. "I haven't seen her in a while. Not since she sold me that love potion that worked a little too well."

Grandma Trini glanced at her watch. "If we hurry, we can catch her before she closes. Doña Lisa always closes for her *novela* hour."

Fabi turned and looked back at the grove. She watched some bees as they buzzed from blossom to blossom down the row of fruit trees. A part of her wanted to stay here. She wanted to be left alone to wallow some more; she wasn't sure she had strength yet to face the world. Maybe a *bruja* was exactly what she needed.

They dropped Alexis and Georgia Rae at home before heading back toward downtown McAllen. It was growing dark and Fabi noticed the bright beams of searchlights shining from the convention center. She didn't say anything, trying to focus on the road ahead, but the thought of Melodee's party slowly crept back into her mind like a daddy longlegs. Was Daniel dancing with Melodee this very second? Were they making out on the dance floor? She couldn't believe that he could do something like that. How could he trick her like that? She had trusted him. Fabi thought he was her friend. She'd opened up to him like she'd opened up to no one else, not even her sister. She'd cried all over his shirt. The memory stung in her chest like heartburn.

They stopped in front of a tiny storefront sandwiched between a used tire shop and a Laundromat with a cartoon washing machine chasing bubbles on the window. The street was deserted except for a mother with three kids pushing a shopping cart full of clothes. Grandma Trini walked to the door and rang the doorbell. The place was called La India Poderosa, the Powerful Indian. Hanging above the doorway was a painting of an Indian woman with a proud dark face, high cheekbones, and slanted eyes. She was holding a feather in one hand and a candle in the other. There was an altar set up in the window. Statues of various saints, candles, dried roses, and gold necklaces adorned the altar. The inside of the shop was hidden behind a heavy velvet curtain. *La India must like her privacy*, Fabi thought. Secretly, she'd always wanted to enter one of these shops, but Abuelita Alpha scared her with stories of devil-worshipping cults stealing bad little girls to mate with *el diablo*. A buzzing sound opened the door and then they stepped in.

Inside, the air was thick with the scent of sandalwood incense, candle wax, and . . . kitty litter. They'd walked into a pharmacy-like store with a long glass counter that took up half of the room. Fabi noticed another curtain dividing the space at the far end. Maybe that's where they did their ceremonies, she wondered. Behind the counter were rows of glass jars with dried herbs. She recognized some of the names: *ruda*, *romero*, horsetail. Those were names of medicinal plants. Abuelita Alpha had a bunch of them growing in front of her house. Whenever Fabi had an earache, her *abuela* would take a bunch of leaves from the *ruda* plant, spit on it, and shove it in her ear.

There were other things there, too, that frightened her. Like the three-foot carved wooden statue of the devil in the corner. It had a rooster claw for one foot and a goat hoof for the other. There were also numerous statues of Saint Death (La Santa Muerte) for sale.

"Trinidad!" a woman cried. Fabi jumped. She hadn't heard anyone enter.

"Doña Lisa!" The two women hugged like old friends.

Doña Lisa had to be ancient. Her wrinkles all over her face looked like they were spun by spiders. She moved with difficulty, as if her knees resisted each step. Her skin was pale and she wore her white hair tied back in a tight bun with sparkly, star-shaped barrettes. The woman did not look powerful, or even Indian.

Grandma Trini explained the situation to the woman in Spanish, told her about Melodee and the bet, the quinceañera that was now probably not going to happen, and the humiliation. It was hard for Fabi to listen. She wished they were talking about someone else, but they weren't. That was her life.

"*Necesitamos un milagro*, a miracle," her grandmother said.

The older woman invited them into her back room. It was the size of a closet, with a round table and a deck of cards. She told them to sit and began to light candles around the room.

When Doña Lisa finally sat down, she asked Fabi to hold out her hand. Fabi hesitated, glancing quickly at her grandmother, who nodded, so Fabi gave the woman her hand. Doña Lisa carefully studied the lines on her palm like a page in a book. Then she huffed and turned to Grandma Trini.

"The girl is cursed." Her eyes flicked over to Fabi and held on like death's grip. "Hate and envy are powerful energies, and this girl really does not like you. Go to the front and grab a bottle of rose water. Use the rose water every day to keep off the bad energy. Tonight, you will take a special bath with herbs I'll prepare for you. Things will get better."

Fabi nodded, getting up stiffly. She'd grown up hearing stories about the evil eye and curses, but she never thought it was real or that it could happen to her. Who would be envious of her? The idea of being cursed scared her more than she cared to admit. Fabi would do whatever the *bruja* said to make it go away.

Grandma Trini didn't move. "Go along, *mija*. I have something more to discuss with Doña Lisa."

Fabi headed to the front of the store and grabbed a bottle of rose water and waited for her grandmother. Twenty minutes later, her grandmother emerged from the back room with a satisfied expression. As Doña Lisa collected the herbs for Fabi's bath she kept looking back to the statue of the devil against the wall.

"Are you sure you want to do this again?" she asked Grandma Trini in Spanish. "The last time you got lucky."

"This is my granddaughter we're talking about. I would do anything for her."

The doorbell chimed. The old woman handed Fabi the bag of herbs. Fabi thanked her.

"I have a feeling that we will be seeing each other very soon, *querida*. Watch out for handsome boys. They are not always what they seem."

Fabi nodded as she left. A tall man with lots of gold chains was waiting at the door. It was Juan "El Payaso" Diamante, the *narcotraficante*. Grandma Trini greeted him politely.

Outside, Fabi touched her grandmother's arm. "That's the guy Santiago was running away from the night he got bit on the butt by the dogs!"

Trini shrugged as she got into her car. "A lot of people come to Doña Lisa for advice."

chapter 11

The cleansing baths didn't make Fabi feel any better, but at least she was clean. When Monday came around, Fabi broke out in hives. She was all too happy to stay home from school — she couldn't imagine facing anyone, especially Melodee and her boyfriend, Daniel. But she had to tell her parents the truth. She spent all morning in bed, trying to come up with the best way to explain. What if the truth made her dad sick again? Her mother now had double hospital bills to worry about.

No, she had to tell them.

At noon, Fabi crawled out of bed and made breakfast. *Huevos a la Mexicana* was her favorite. There was extra for her dad.

His face lit up when she walked into his bedroom with a tray. Fabi noticed the walker that he refused to use. He needed to walk, like the doctor prescribed. But her dad was also really stubborn and didn't like change.

"Wow, *mija*, you made this?" Leonardo said, looking at the scrambled eggs with green jalapeño chilies, onion, and tomatoes.

"I learned from the best."

He took a bite, and then another. His eyes grew big. "This is real good."

"And good *for* you," Fabi added. "I used extra virgin olive oil, and the vegetables are from Grandpa Frank's garden. They're organic."

Her dad didn't say anything. Munching softly, he closed his eyes to let the flavors sink in and swirl in his mouth. Then he opened his eyes and said, "When I get back to the restaurant I want you to start working with me in the kitchen."

"Really?"

"Of course, *mi changuita*." He pinched her cheek lovingly. "Maybe you can teach this old dog some new organic tricks," he added with a wink.

Fabi beamed. She was touched — and she could see he was in a good mood. This was the moment she'd been waiting for. "So, Dad, there's something I need to tell you about the quinceañera."

He sat up. Leonardo had lost a lot of weight since his heart attack. She didn't like to see her dad like this. He looked so fragile and vulnerable, but she had to tell him the quince was off.

But before she could speak, her father said, "Good. There's something I've been meaning to tell you, too. Being in the hospital gave me a lot of time to think. I thought a lot about my life and the things I'm grateful for. I'm sorry I couldn't provide you with a proper quinceañera —"

"No, Dad —"

"Let me finish." Leonardo put his plate to the side and looked her in the eyes. "Maybe this *ataque* was a good thing. I've been working too hard, trying to run everything by myself. I've missed out on so much of your life, and look at you now, all grown up and feeding me." A tear jerked from his big dark eye. "I'm so grateful that your sister and grandmother were able to get you this opportunity, *mija*. Who cares who serves the food and whether it's any good. The important thing is that you get the fiesta that you deserve."

"Dad." Fabi's chest tightened with emotion.

"I'm so proud of you. I love you so much," he said, and pulled her into a hug.

Tears welled up in Fabi's eyes as she pulled away. She didn't know what to say.

"You're becoming a beautiful woman and I can't believe that you're mine. Now, what did you want to tell me?"

Fabi stared at him. How could she break his heart? "It's nothing." She wiped away her tears. "I'm just so happy that you're feeling better and will be there for my special day."

"I wouldn't miss it for the world."

Fabi got up to let him rest. He had a beautiful smile on his lips when she closed the door behind her. What was she going to do? she wondered, her anxiety rising. Fabi started to clean the kitchen. Cleaning always helped her think. Her quinceañera was scheduled for Saturday, and she hadn't heard a word from Grace since Melodee's party. Was Grace already back on a plane to L.A.?

By Wednesday, the hives had blistered up and her mom threatened to drag her to the doctor if she didn't get better. After school, Alexis brought Fabi's homework so she wouldn't fall behind. People were asking for her. They wanted to know if the party was still going to happen.

The sun was just starting to set when there was a knock at the door. Fabi answered it in her pajamas. It was Grace Cooper. The surprise visit shook Fabi, and without thinking, she slammed the door closed. Fabi leaned against the wood, heart beating wildly. Her body was so tense she could barely breathe.

Grace knocked on the door. "Fabi," she said shyly. "Can I come in?"

There was no hiding now. Fabi took a deep breath. Her face was hot and she started to feel dizzy. But she had to face up to her actions. Grace wore a blank expression when Fabi opened the door a second time. She looked cool and collected in her black business suit, frilly blouse, and black pumps.

Fabi led her into the modest living room. She was a little embarrassed because she knew her house wasn't glamorous — most of the furniture was secondhand.

"I'm sorry I didn't call before," Grace said. "I've been having a lot of meetings with the show's producers and this was the first chance I got to come over."

Fabi curled up in a ball on the opposite side of the couch. Grace smiled sadly at her, then looked down at the floor.

"That was quite a shocker we all got at Melodee's quinceañera," she said.

Fabi looked down, unable to raise her eyes.

"I talked to Alexis and your grandmother," Grace went on. "They explained everything about the letter." She took a deep breath. "By contract, we have to cancel this episode. We take fraud very seriously, you know? And you're obligated to pay for all expenses we've incurred."

Fabi nodded sadly, surrendering to her responsibilities.

"But . . ."

Fabi looked up.

"I was able to convince my producers that we had to do this show. With your dad's heart attack and the great lengths your family made to provide this opportunity, it gave me an idea." Grace reached out to Fabi, putting a manicured hand on her knee. "I know what it's like to feel inadequate, to feel less than, because your family is low income."

"You do?" Fabi couldn't believe what she was hearing.

"Yeah. My family didn't have money when I was your age. I never even had a quinceañera. I know I don't look it, but my mom's Dominican. Quinceañeras are a big deal in the Dominican community. My parents couldn't afford a fancy party and I didn't want my friends to laugh at me. I lied to my friends at school and told them that I didn't want one and that my parents were sending me to Paris instead." Grace laughed as if the whole thing was ridiculous. "I was ashamed of my family. It's hard to admit now, because I love them dearly. They worked hard and did without a lot of things so that I could get a good education and go to college. My parents were both illegal immigrants: My father was from Ireland and my mother was from a small ranch in the Dominican Republic. They met at a restaurant where my mom cooked and my dad was a waiter. Like you and your family, we didn't have a lot of money growing up, but we had heart."

Fabi stared at Grace Cooper in shock. This fabulous, sophisticated woman used to be like her. It made Fabi's heart swell and she liked her even more.

"Since they gave me this project, I decided that I was going to continue it. But it's no longer about a girl who is dying. The show is about a healthy American girl and the family that loves her."

"Really?"

Grace nodded. "Fabi, I don't think you realize how special you really are. There're a ton of girls out there who, because of the way they look, where their parents are from, or their economic status, don't think they're special enough. I'm tired of my bosses and their demands for high ratings. That's not the spirit of the quinceañera and not why I took this job."

"Really?" Fabi repeated in disbelief.

"Really," Grace said with conviction. "The party is still set for Saturday, if you're still interested."

Fabi didn't know what to say. This was so unexpected. Was this a dream?

"Yes," a voice said behind her. Fabi and Grace both turned to see Leonardo standing in the hallway. "Fabi will have her day."

Tears sprang to Fabi's eyes and she smiled brightly at her dad. She didn't care anymore if he knew about the lie. She didn't care if the whole world knew the truth. "Yes," Fabi said to Grace. "I'll do it."

"Good," Grace said, and leaned in to Fabi. "Besides, between you and me, I don't want Melodee to have the last word. I hate bullies, and she is a *queen* bully if you ask me."

Fabi pressed her lips together for a moment. "She's been a thorn in my side ever since freshman year."

"Well then, it's settled. I need you back in school tomorrow for a couple of new shots we need to take. Can we meet at lunch?"

"Of course."

Grace got up to leave. At the door Fabi was overwhelmed with appreciation and gave her a big hug. Grace beamed back. "You don't have to thank me. I'm just glad I was here to make this happen."

When Saturday finally came, Fabi couldn't calm the butterflies bouncing around in her stomach. Grace was doing a great job of coordinating all the details, but Fabi still didn't have a *chambelán*. Santiago offered to step in, but Grandma Trini told them not to worry; she'd already taken care of it.

The plan was for everyone to come over to Fabi's house to get ready. Grace had arranged for a hair and makeup artist to help. Now Fabi glanced at the quince party, sitting around the makeshift dressing room that used to be her kitchen. Alexis was sitting on a stool at the counter. Her hair was in rollers and she was smiling with her face tilted up as the makeup artist painted her eyelids. Grandma Trini was making some last-minute "improvements" to her dress — lowering the neckline so her bosom had air to breathe. Santiago was hogging the bathroom. He was worse then Grandma Trini when it came to gelling his curls.

Fabi felt a pang of sadness that Milo hadn't shown up. *He must still be sore*, she thought. But she didn't know how to make things right with him. Thankfully, Chuy was about Milo's size, so he fit perfectly in his suit. Fabi couldn't help but notice how cute he looked in a tux.

Grace walked in, texting on her BlackBerry. She'd been running back and forth from the hall to the house all morning, making sure nothing went wrong. Fabi was so happy to have met her. She was the supreme quinceañera coordinator and kept everyone on time.

And then Grandma Trini informed everyone of the latest addition to the party.

"A surprise *chambelán*!" Grace smiled approvingly. "I love it. Who is it? No, wait, don't tell me. I want to be surprised, too."

"Who is this guy?" Fabi asked; she couldn't help but be worried. Her grandmother had a knack for making situations even bigger. But her grandmother wouldn't budge. Fabi prayed that nothing bad would happen today. One day, that's all she wanted. One day with nothing bad happening.

Fabi chose a classic updo with curly tresses. It was a fun, sophisticated look, she decided. She gathered her dress, shoes, gloves, and tiara and kicked Santiago out of the bathroom to change. She loved the feel of the silk dress fabric on her skin. The dress was her favorite color, turquoise. Fabi had originally wanted a simple, classic gown that she could wear to other events. But when she saw the strapless gown with the sparkly green and orange beaded floral design on the bodice and the soft billowy full-length skirt, she fell in love. The dress was a little snug around the waist, but the designer swore that all of the gowns fit that way.

With her tiara and favorite checked sneakers on, she was ready to go. Fabi glanced, with hesitation, at the pretty stiletto heels that Grandma Trini had convinced her to get for the shoe-changing ceremony. She didn't quite understand why she had to give up her sneakers for a pair of uncomfortable heels. It was a rite of passage, her grandmother swore. But Fabi knew that Grandma Trini really just wanted to borrow the heels someday, since they wore the same size.

"This is it," Fabi said to herself as she opened the bathroom door. She took a deep breath. Would people think she was pretty?

The kitchen erupted when she walked in.

"Woo-hoo!"

"Yeah!"

"Que guapa!"

Everyone cheered as she twirled around. Fabi could feel her face growing hot. But she couldn't help but admit it felt good to be the star today.

"All right, everybody," Grace called out from the door. "We need to all be in the car heading to the church in ten minutes."

Abuelita Alpha demanded no music or even laughing in the rented Hummer limo on the way to church for Mass. She also made sure that she sat next to Fabi. She wanted her to focus on the prayers she'd learned and her commitments to the church. If it were up to Fabi's *abuelita*, there would be no party. To her, the quinceañera was all about Fabi's relationship with God. As her grandmother prayed loudly for her, Fabi couldn't help but wish Melodee had a grandmother like hers.

During the Mass, Fabi was worried that she would make a mistake, forget her lines, or fall, but the service went smoothly, much to her *abuelita*'s surprise.

After the priest's blessing, it was time to celebrate. They were finally allowed to play music in the Hummer, and Georgia Rae put on one of Milo's CDs. Alexis raised the volume to full blast. Milo's music made Fabi a little sad. She missed him, but Fabi had to bury her feelings and put on a happy face. Especially since the rest of the limo was having a blast dancing and sipping sweet tea out of champagne glasses. Grandma Trini kept standing up and poking her head out of the sunroof. It was a lot of fun.

When they stopped in front of the Spanish-style 1920s hotel in downtown Weslaco, Fabi was beside herself with excitement. There was a line of guests that went around the block. There had to be over a hundred people there. Grace was tight with security and wanted to make sure that only invited guests were allowed in. Fabi loved having the security guards checking everybody's purses. It made the whole event feel exclusive. The limo door opened and she stepped out. Fabi was greeted with cheers and the flashing lights of cameras. She felt like a rock star.

Inside, the hotel was amazing. It was an old hacienda-style building that had recently been restored to its original design. Fabi's party was the first event hosted there. Beautiful crystal chandeliers lined the hallway that led to the massive hall. The first thing she saw was the quinceañera table, with elegant china and bright-colored dahlias. At the far end of the hall was a grand stage area. A big Target banner hung off the stage area, but Fabi didn't mind. She beamed with gratitude at Grace, who was watching her reaction from the other side of the room.

The crowd of guests filed in and took seats at the empty tables. Fabi saw the school librarian and her husband; the city councilman with his family; her uncles and cousins from Minnesota and California; her elementary school teachers; everyone from school. It seemed like the entire town had shown up.

The event began with the classic song "De Niña a Mujer," performed by the Dos Rios school mariachi band and sung by her sister, Alexis. Fabi's chest tightened with emotion when she thought about how it was her baby sister's crazy love for her that had made all of this possible. She was so proud of her. Tears burst forward when her dad slowly walked onto the dance floor without his walker. He looked so handsome and proud in his cowboy hat, Western tuxedo, and pointy snakeskin boots. They danced slowly. Fabi was cautious of her dad's fragile state. But she was also overwhelmed with emotion. His face beamed as he twirled her. Alexis's voice cracked as she sang. Fabi looked over her shoulder and noticed that there wasn't a dry eye in the crowd.

After the dance Fabi sat at the quinceañera table to eat while the mariachis played all her favorite songs. Fabi didn't realize how hungry she was until the plate of chicken mole with rice and beans appeared in front of her.

"Happy birthday," a voice said behind her. Fabi turned and saw Milo dressed in a slick navy suit with a ruffled shirt.

"You came," she cried, jumping out of her seat to give him a big hug.

"I couldn't possibly miss your big day," he said, blushing.

"Sit here," she said, motioning to the seat next to her. "Sit. Are you my surprise *chambelán*?" she asked hopefully.

Milo's face turned red. "I, uh, no, but I'd —" He glanced around.

Fabi swallowed her pride and grabbed Milo's

hand. "I feel real bad about everything that happened between us."

"So do I," Milo said in a hushed whisper.

"I don't know what I was thinking about Daniel."

He covered her hand with his. "Fabi, can we just forget about the whole thing? I feel bad about a lot of things, too, but let's just put it behind us and enjoy this party."

"Done!"

"Look," Georgia Rae cut in, leaning over and pointing to the entrance.

Walking in, arm in arm, were Melodee and Daniel. Melodee wore a cute cocktail dress, but the big scowl on her face ruined her look. Daniel looked uncomfortable, like he didn't want to be there. Fabi couldn't help but wish things had turned out differently between them. But she refused to be sad. Not on this day. This party was just as nice as Melodee's, if not better. Now, where was her date?

Then Grandma Trini came sauntering over with a gorgeous model-type man on her arm. The man looked like he'd walked off an Italian runway, with his piercing good looks and healthy dark tan. This had to be her surprise *chambelán*, Fabi thought.

"Look what Grandma brought you," Trini said, clapping excitedly. "Happy birthday, *mija*. I want to introduce you to your *chambelán*, Orlando Russo."

The very sexy man shot her a dazzling smile as he kissed her hand. Fabi's cheeks reddened. She had a gazillion questions to ask, but she was interrupted by Grace.

Grace Cooper took the mic and invited everyone to have a seat. She looked beautiful in her green gown. "I'd like to thank everyone for coming here today to celebrate Fabiola Garza's quinceañera."

The guests went wild, cheering for her. Fabi smiled brightly. This was the best day ever, no doubt about it. She waved at her parents, who sat elegantly at the family table with Abuelita Alpha, Grandpa Frank, and her *tía* Consuelo.

"Before we begin with the party," Grace continued, "I'd like to show a little video we made throughout the last couple of weeks. I've produced many quinceañera shows, but this one has by far been the most surprising, and the one I am most proud of. There are so many people to thank who made this day possible, but most importantly I would like to give a special thank-you to Leonardo and Magdalena Garza for raising such a beautiful, proud, and special young girl." Fabi's parents stood and the guests clapped loudly. Grace smiled at Fabi. "And who is Fabiola Garza? Well, just watch this video." She gestured to her assistant, and a wall-sized screen came down from the ceiling.

Fabi saw clips of her appearing on the screen. There were pictures of her walking in the school hallway, working at the restaurant, and studying in the library. Fabi turned to her sister with excitement. This was just too cool.

Then the film cut to her classmates. Violet, Mona, and Noelia talked animatedly about being in the quinceañera. Milo's face lit up the screen. He brought up the time Fabi had taught him how to barbecue. Georgia Rae recounted the time Fabi ran around the *raspa* stand wearing camouflage paint and scared some customers away. Then Daniel appeared on the screen. The video must have been made before his public betrayal. Fabi held her breath and tried not to notice his beautiful dimples. Daniel said Fabi was a great person, with a real big heart and a pretty smile. His words made her uncomfortable. She wished they'd edited him out.

Next came Chuy, and Fabi sighed with relief. Chuy thanked her for all the times she helped him with his English. Her grandpa Frank told the story about when Fabi was five and she'd finished a whole box of chocolate-flavored Ex-Lax. He'd been so scared that he raced her to the doctor to get her stomach pumped. The crowd loved that story and laughed really hard. Then Abuelita Alpha brought everyone to tears with her story of Fabiola playing the baby Jesus when she was two in the church play.

The best interview, though, was her dad's. He was standing in the restaurant's kitchen as he recounted his "little *changuita*" following him around when he cooked. It was the old Leonardo, the one before the heart attack. He looked so strong and healthy. He told the story of when he put chili on Fabi's fingertips so she would stop sucking her thumb. Fabi's heart swelled. Of course, it hadn't worked, because then Fabi just got into the habit of sucking her chili-flavored thumb. Fabi laughed with the guests at that. She turned and smiled at her dad.

"You are one lucky girl," the handsome guest *chambelán* said, sliding into the empty seat next to Fabi.

Fabi was speechless for a second. The stranger had the softest light brown eyes with little gold specks. She couldn't help but melt into them. Fabi secretly hoped Daniel was noticing this handsome man talking to her.

"I am," she said. "I feel like the luckiest girl in the world."

He smiled. "Your grandmother Trinidad told me all about you. I'm so honored to be your date tonight."

Fabi giggled with delight. She didn't care how much her grandmother had paid him. He was so beautiful.

Fabi went through all of the traditional ceremonial rites: *La Última Muñeca*, the father-daughter dance, and the changing of the shoes. That was the hardest part, because she hadn't had a chance to practice walking in the stilettos. But she followed her Grandma Trini's advice and faked it. When it was time to cut the cake, Santiago couldn't resist shoving Fabi's face into the cake as the crowd cheered her to take a bite. Fabi tried to be mad, but the audience was laughing and cheering so hard she decided to return the favor, and smashed the remainder of the cake piece on Santiago's face.

The lights dimmed for the highlight of the evening, the quinceañera dance. Everyone did their best. Fabi kept forgetting which direction to turn. Was it left or right? Thankfully, Orlando was like a dream and led her beautifully. He knew all the choreography, as if he'd been practicing alongside them in all of the practices. Fabi couldn't remember a time when she was happier. Then the professional reggaeton band came out and the crowd went crazy on the dance floor.

A line of guests wanted to dance with Fabi. She made an effort to dance at least once with everyone. As she two-stepped with Grandpa Frank around the dance floor she noticed Daniel making his way toward her.

Fabi craned her neck to be sure. Off to the left stood Melodee. She was calling out to Daniel, shouting angrily. But Daniel ignored her and continued pushing through the crowd. Her pulse jumped. What did he want? Grandpa

Frank whirled her again when Daniel arrived. He nodded at Daniel. Fabi wanted to stop her grandpa, but he was already heading to the buffet table.

"Hey, Fabi," Daniel said, standing just a foot away from her. He was so close she could smell his peppermint gum. He did look cute, she thought.

But he's a liar, she reminded herself. *A jerk. And Melodee's boyfriend!*

"Hey," she said back, with indifference.

"Nice party."

She glanced around, waiting for someone to save her.

Daniel glanced quickly over his shoulder. "I, um . . . I wanted to . . . um . . . I'm really sorry. About everything."

Fabi rolled her eyes. *Now* he was sorry?

"I meant that stuff that I said, you know, to the camera," Daniel went on, stuttering a little less now. "I think you're an amazing girl. I never wanted for any of this to happen. I just didn't expect you to be so cool, you know? I thought . . ."

"Princesa," Orlando interrupted, sliding in between them. "They're playing our song."

Fabi shot Daniel a smug shrug. Orlando was so great! Daniel and Melodee could eat her dust, Fabi thought as she turned into Orlando's waiting arms.

Orlando smiled at Daniel and then said, "Your loss."

Fabi leaned her head back and laughed. Orlando was perfect in so many ways, she didn't know where to begin. Daniel moved to the sidelines. He watched with a pained expression.

Across the dance floor, Abuelita Alpha was dancing with Grandma Trini. Abuelita Alpha couldn't take her eyes off of Orlando. There was something about him that she didn't like. "Where did he come from?"

Grandma Trini shook her shoulders roughly. "He's an old friend of mine."

"An old friend?"

Grandma Trini just smiled slyly as she twirled in place.

"Is he a male escort?"

Grandma Trini opened her mouth in shock and made a swatting gesture. "Don't say that. No, he's not, and don't start any rumors. Fabi needed a handsome *chambelán* to make that rich girl eat her dust."

Abuelita Alpha stared at Trini.

"Don't give me that look, either," Trini said, shaking her hips. "You weren't there. You didn't hear the mean things that girl said about our Fabiola."

"You still can't forgive those girls who used to tease you back in our days?"

"Water under the bridge. I've already forgotten about that. I can't believe you still remember."

Abuelita Alpha turned back to Orlando. "There's something about him that looks familiar," she murmured.

"Don't even think about ruining this party with your speculations. I've never seen Fabi so happy. *Déjala gozar.* Just this one time."

Fabi didn't hear the conversation, nor did she notice her *abuelita*'s disapproving stare. She was having too much fun dancing with Orlando. He was such a good dancer she felt like she was floating on air. The sips of champagne must have been going to her head because she could barely feel the floor below her feet as they glided across it. She heard people gasping in awe. The dance classes made her feel so much more comfortable with her body that she didn't even turn. In Orlando's arms she knew they looked good. *It's a dream come true*, she thought, allowing the bliss to consume her as he whirled her faster and faster around.

All of a sudden a straw broom smacked her on the back. Fabi shook in surprise. The blows hit her and Orlando again and again. Fabi looked behind her and saw Abuelita Alpha with a raised broom in her hands, aiming for another strike. Grandma Trini was pulling at Abuelita's sweater, trying to get her to stop. But Alpha had gone mad.

"¡Lágarte, diablo maldito!" Abuelita Alpha screamed with feverish venom. Where was the security? Fabi wanted to cry for help.

With godly strength, Alpha shook Grandma Trini off her. Trini fell back and into the crowd. Fabi couldn't believe it. Her head felt fuzzy from all the twirls. She shook her head to clear it. Then, Fabi fell flat on her butt on the hard wooden floor. Abuelita Alpha continued swinging the broom like it was a bat at Orlando, cursing up a storm. Fabi was shocked; she didn't know her *abuelita* even knew those words.

Orlando glared angrily at Abuelita Alpha. Her grandmother was out of control. Fabi tried to get up and stop this, but her dress was too big and puffy.

"Stop, Alpha!" Trini yelled from the crowd. "You'll ruin everything!"

"Security!" Fabi shouted. There was no way she was going to let her grandmother ruin her party. Not now! Not when it was going so well. But nobody moved. Were they all just as shocked as her?

Orlando stepped back, blocking the blows with his arm. He had edged back to the windows. Her *chambelán* was trapped, and Alpha continued after him as if he was some hunted animal. Fabi's *abuelita* raised the broom high over her head and Orlando turned to Fabi. He blew her a kiss, and then jumped through the window.

Fabi screamed. There was a crash, and shards of broken glass went everywhere. This was horrible. Fabi rolled onto her knees. Alexis was at her side and helped her up.

"What was that?" Alexis cried.

Fabi shook her head. They ran to the window, where their *abuelita* was standing with a smug look on her face. Fabi leaned out the broken window and noticed the drop. It had to be at least three stories. But it was dark outside and there was no sign of Orlando. No one could make that jump without breaking something, she thought. But he was gone. It was as if he just disappeared into the night.

"Abuelita," Fabi cried, close to hysterics. "What did you do?"

Her grandmother made the sign of the cross in front of her. "I'm sorry, *mija*. I had to do it."

"Abuelita, he was my *chambelán*! You can't be doing that."

"I had to," her *abuelita* stated again confidently. "He was the devil."

Fabi couldn't believe her grandmother's crazy antics. This was too far! "No, he wasn't. He was a nice guy. He was just helping me out."

"No, *mija*." Her grandmother shook her head sadly. "That was *el diablo*. I swear on my life, that was him. You don't know better because you're so young and vulnerable. But I know. At first I was trying to see his legs. The devil can't transform his feet, you know?" She made hand gestures as if that would help. "He has one that looks like a rooster's claw and the other is like one of Grandpa's goat's cloven hooves. But then I saw you both dancing and swirling."

"That's how people dance nowadays." Fabi was exhausted and definitely didn't have the energy to explain current dance trends to her grandmother.

"*Mija*, you two were spinning. Spinning above the floor in the air. If I didn't break the spell, he would have spirited you away into hell. Is that what you want, you ungrateful child? Next time I'll let him take you!"

Fabi groaned in frustration. There was no talking to her grandmother when she got like this. Nothing was going to convince her otherwise. Fabi turned back to the party. Everyone was staring at her in shock. She shrugged.

"He had to go," she said to the crowd. Fabi sighed. Well, at least it wasn't a total disaster, she thought as the next *cumbia* came on and everyone started to dance again. Milo came up to her and asked her to dance. Fabi headed back to the packed dance floor. This time she made sure she kept her feet firmly on the floor.

epilogue

That night became known as the night Fabi danced with the devil. Fabi wondered how much her *abuelita* Alpha had to do with the rumor, but she let it slide. Enough had happened that made her want to put the whole quince fight behind her.

Grace went back to Los Angeles. The show would air in a couple of months, once they finished editing the footage. She was going to call Fabi when it was ready. Grace also invited Fabi to Los Angeles over the summer break. Her dad promised to think about it.

At school, Fabi found that her celebrity status disappeared when the camera's lights went out. She was glad that things were back to normal.

Well, almost — Santiago punched Daniel in the hallway right in front of the vice principal's office. They suspended him, but Santiago didn't care. He said he was done with pretending to be a schoolboy.

Melodee demanded a do-over because she said Fabi cheated. A rumor circulated that Fabi's *chambelán* was a hired escort and thus she broke the rules.

"What rules?" Fabi asked. "There are no quinceañera rules."

Melodee fumed, "The *rules*! Everyone knows that you can't hire someone to be your *chambelán*. That's cheating."

"Well, you cheated, too," Fabi snapped back. "You told Daniel to get close to me so that I'd ask him to be my *chambelán*, when you knew he was your boyfriend. That makes the whole bet null and void."

"Fine," Melodee spat.

"Fine."

Melodee spun around without another word and walked away, her crew trailing behind like a long piece of toilet paper attached to her shoe.

Alexis laughed out loud. Fabi and Milo

joined in with her. Everything seemed to be back to normal.

Later that day, Fabi and Santiago returned to the hall to pick up Fabi's Vans. The evening had been so crazy she'd forgotten her shoes under the quinceañera table. Fabi still wondered about Orlando. Grandma Trini refused to utter a word about him. She wouldn't say where he lived or even tell her how to reach him.

They walked around the ground underneath the window where Orlando had jumped, looking for signs of him. Fabi was looking for some kind of evidence, like maybe a wallet. Orlando, like everything else she'd experienced the last couple of months (Melodee, Daniel, and *Quince Dreams*), felt like someone else's memory. It was hard to believe she was the eye of this storm. A small smile danced on her lips. *The last couple of months were kind of cool in a weird, my-family's-crazy kind of way*, she thought. Daniel was still a sore spot for her. Had there been a sliver of truth to what he said at her party? she wondered.

Poor Orlando must think she had a schizo

family. How could her *abuelita* attack her *chambelán* like that? The area under the window was clear — except for some empty chip wrappers and beer bottles.

"Hey, look at this," Santiago said, pointing at an indentation in the dirt.

"What is that?" Fabi asked, kneeling down for a closer look.

"They look like some kind of prints," he said, using his finger to trace an outline.

"They don't look like footprints."

Fabi stared, trying to think of what could have made those prints in the dirt directly under the window Orlando had jumped from. Then it hit her. They looked just like the hoof-prints Grandpa Frank's goat made in the mud in the corral. Well, at least, one of them did. The other print was a long line, with two shorter lines poking out, like a triangle.

"Hey, that's a chicken footprint," Santiago said. "Didn't Abuelita Alpha say something about the devil's feet . . ."

"No." Fabi started to laugh. "It can't be . . . could it?" *Could Orlando really be the devil?* she wondered. But if he was the devil, why did he help her? Didn't the devil have bigger people to fry? She was nobody. And how come her grandmothers knew him? No, Orlando was not the devil, she thought. In the Valley, the real devils were the *narcotraficantes* murdering innocent people, giving kids guns, and spreading violence on the other side of the border.

Just then a black Escalade with tinted windows pulled up alongside them and parked. Fabi held her breath as El Payaso Diamante stepped out of the vehicle. Had she willed the *narcotraficante* to appear with her thoughts? Santiago stood as stiff as a statue next to her. She could sense his fear, like a rabbit caught in a hunter's trap. This couldn't be good.

The husky man with salt-and-pepper hair and a fat gold medallion on his chest walked up to them. Fabi's eye glanced around for an escape route.

"Santiago Reyes," El Payaso said in a raspy authoritative voice. Fabi and Santiago swallowed at the same time. "I hear you changed."

"Yes, sir," Santiago stuttered.

"I hear you're going to school and staying away from the girls and the business. I hear you even made a promise to La Virgen. Is that right?"

Santiago glanced sideways at Fabi with a surprised expression before answering, "Yes, sir. I did. But how did . . ."

El Payaso waved Santiago's question away. "A promise to Our Lady del Valle is not something to take lightly. Have you gone to the *Santuario* to make an offering?"

Santiago's eyes got real wide. "I, um, I . . ."

"I thought so." El Payaso looked down at his boots. "You better get on it."

"Yes, sir." Santiago nodded quickly.

"I'll be watching you, Santiago. I'll be watching your grades, your after-school activities. If I hear that you're messing with any girls or in any dealings, I will be on you like hell's wrath. I let you go because *mi hija* likes you and I made a promise not to harm a hair on your pretty little head, as long as you stay in line. *¿Entiendes, menso?*"

"I understand, sir," Santiago answered.

"Now, get over to *El Santuario* and thank La Virgen before I change my mind," El Payaso said threateningly.

Without answering, Santiago grabbed Fabi's hand and pulled her down the alleyway, away from El Payaso. They ran hard, as if they were running from the devil himself. Neither one of them spoke. Life in the Valley was full of surprises. As they ran away, Fabi realized that they both had a lot to be thankful for. They had their health, their family, and luck on their side. Someone was definitely watching over them. Was it La Virgen or someone else? Whoever it was, Fabi was thankful for their protection and made a promise to take a bouquet of flowers to Our Lady of San Juan del Valle's shrine, just in case.